LENNY HENRY

THE QUEST FOR THE BIG WOOF

ILLUSTRATED BY STEVE PARKHOUSE

PENGUIN BOOKS

PENGUIN BOOKS

Published by the Penguin Group
Penguin Books Ltd, 27 Wrights Lane, London W8 5TZ, England
Penguin Books USA Inc., 375 Hudson Street, New York, New York 10014, USA
Penguin Books Australia Ltd, Ringwood, Victoria, Australia
Penguin Books Canada Ltd, 10 Alcorn Avenue, Toronto, Ontario, Canada M4V 3B2
Penguin Books (NZ) Ltd, 182–190 Wairau Road, Auckland 10, New Zealand

Penguin Books Ltd, Registered Offices: Harmondsworth, Middlesex, England

First published in Penguin Books 1991
10 9 8 7 6 5 4 3 2 1

Origination by Anglia Graphics Ltd, Bedford
Printed in England by William Clowes Limited, Beccles

Introduction

Oh, great.

Us comic creators spend ten years trying to teach the general public that just because they're called "comics", that doesn't mean that they're necessarily comical. We even tried getting people to call comics "Graphic Novels", which, you'll admit, sounds about as un-comedic as they come. I mean, we really put a lot of sweat into this re-educating the masses thing, and what happens?

I find myself writing the introduction for a comical comic book written by a comic, that's what bloody happens. And now nobody knows what to call the bloody things and we'll probably have to start all over again and I don't think I can take it. Not another ten years of magazine articles titled "Bam! Sock! Pow! The Comic Grows Up." I just can't, that's all.

On the other hand, since the book in question is such a sterling piece of work, how can I shirk my responsibilities? And, to be fair, he *did* have Delbert Wilkins mention *Swamp Thing* once, although he was noticeably cool towards my suggestion that I should make a number of light-hearted cameo appearances on the show, followed by a possible zany spin-off mini-series. Still, forgive and forget.

The trouble is, how does one go about writing an introduction for a work as individual as *The Big Woof*? Should I go for the scholarly approach and do that bit about "the formal melding of image and text" which I think I still have written on my shirt sleeve from one of those BBC 2 arts programmes? Or should I go for whacky? Or sort of basically scholarly but a bit whacky round the edges, like Bamber Gascoigne on animal tranquillizers?

It's probably safest, all things considered, to start with a description: *The Big Woof* is what happens when you take a very talented and funny individual who's been a comic fan longer than he's been a comic, team him up with one of the finest and most versatile comic-book artists in the business, and then get him to talk about all the things closest to his heart. Like comedy, comic books, cosmic odysseys in the company of the Almighty. That sort of stuff.

And, it must be said, he's very good at it. Certainly a lot better than I'd be at convulsing packed houses with my impression of an elderly Jamaican, that's for sure. In *The Big Woof*, Lenny takes everything he's learned and everything he's loved about comics, and expertly applies it to an extended meditation upon the rigours and responsibilities of his day job. In between all the thigh-slappers and aisle-rollers, he also manages to ask a very serious question, a question that must have been muttered in tones of haunted despair by anyone who's ever tried to write anything even mildly amusing to a deadline: "What's funny?"

Of course, it should be pointed out that he's had some expert assistance in this. Steve Parkhouse, artistic luminary behind the visually delightful and, frankly, stunningly written "Bojeffries Saga", is a consummate professional of the first water, able to tell a story in pictures with perfect clarity while shifting through a range of styles unequalled since Dudley Watkins and the classic British comic artists of the fifties and sixties. In an attempt to conquer *The Big Woof*, you couldn't hope for a better sherpa.

All in all, what you have in your hand is a very funny and strikingly handsome volume where two extraordinary talents come together to produce something that is an excellent piece of comic story-telling, however you choose to define the term. I just hope it doesn't start a trend. If this time next year I find myself writing the introduction to "Frankie Howerd's JUDGE DREDD" ("Titter ye not, creep, I am the Law.") then I may well end up regretting the whole business.

Until then, pull up a chair, turn down the tweeters, and enjoy *The Big Woof*.

Alan Moore
Northampton 1991

OUR STORY BEGINS SOMEWHERE HEAVENWARD...
COMEDY...
IS A DELIGHTFUL EXTRAVAGANCE.
WE GET DEPRESSED...
THE JERK
TOMMY COOPE
The MARX BR
ELYSIUM PIZZA
GROUCHO MARX WAGGLES A PAINTED EYEBROW.
CHOMP
THE BUCK · STOPS · HERE
JOHN BELUSHI SPEWS MASHED POTATO AND SHOUTS "SEE, I'M A ZIT! A **ZIT**, GEDDIT?"
CHAPLIN GASSES A TOUGH IN 'EASY STREET'...

"AND WE CHUCKLE, GIGGLE, GUFFAW—LOSE TOTAL CONTROL OF OUR BODILY FUNCTIONS."
"IT'S A PARTICULARLY HUMAN TRAIT, LAUGHTER. YOU DON'T SEE ELEPHANTS WALKING AROUND SNIGGERING TO THEMSELVES."
NOW THIS GUY IS REALLY FUNNY. HE CAN MAKE YOU SQUIRT MILK DOWN YOUR NOSE. NOT A LOT OF PEOPLE CAN DO THAT.
"OF COURSE, THERE ARE OTHER LIFEFORMS DOTTED AROUND THE COSMOS WITH THE GIFT FOR COMEDY...
"BUT NONE SO HIGHLY DEVELOPED AS HUMANKIND..."
"I SUPPOSE CIRCUMSTANCES COME INTO IT..."
"THE EARTH IS NOT AN EASY PLACE TO INHABIT..."
"NO 'OUTING TO BLACKPOOL' AS SOME MIGHT PUT IT..."
"YET THROUGH IT ALL, THE 6-DAY WAR, CUBAN MISSILE CRISIS, WORLD WAR ONE, WORLD WAR TWO, HIROSHIMA, VIETNAM, THALIDOMIDE CHILDREN, THIRD WORLD FAMINE, HOMELESSNESS..."
"AND THE CONTINUING RISE OF STOCK, AITKEN AND WATERMAN..."

"COMEDY SEEMS TO BE THE GREAT HEALER.
ONE OF THEM, ANYWAY."
"AND COMEDIANS WRITE, PRODUCE, PERFORM... SELFLESSLY GIVING PLEASURE TO OTHERS...
THOUGH THE CREATION OF COMEDY DOESN'T REALLY BEAR CLOSE SCRUTINY...
DISSECT IT, AND THE SUBJECT DIES..."
"LIKE A MATINEE PERFORMANCE AT THE NORTH PIER THEATRE IN BLACKPOOL..."
SPERLATT!
"OR THE GRAVEYARD SHIFT AT 'CORLEONE'S BUMP AND GRIND' SALOON IN THE BRONX."
"IT'S JUST SOMETHING YOU WOULDN'T WANT TO SEE...
NOT CLOSE UP, ANYWAY."
"I BELIEVE COMEDY IS ESSENTIAL TO THE SURVIVAL OF MAN— LAUGHTER IS THERAPEUTIC."
(SEE PAGE 79 OF 'IT'S A FACT' BY GYLES BRANDRETH, PUBLISHED BY NOBHEAD PRESS.)
"SO IF A COMEDIAN NEEDS INSPIRATION, IT WOULD BE UNKIND NOT TO PROVIDE A LITTLE NUDGE IN THE RIGHT DIRECTION—
BECAUSE SOMETIMES...
COMEDIANS NEED ALL THE HELP THEY CAN GET..."
TIME, I THINK...
CLIK!
FOR A LITTLE...
"INTERVENTION."
BOF!
WHO YA GONNA CALL—?

FIRST PULSE-POUNDING ISH IN THIS PEERLESS PENGUIN PURSUIT OF...
THE BIG WOOF
No.1
10¢
WHERE'S THE BLOODY WOOF THEN?
Parkhouse '91
MY NAME IS LENNY HENRY...

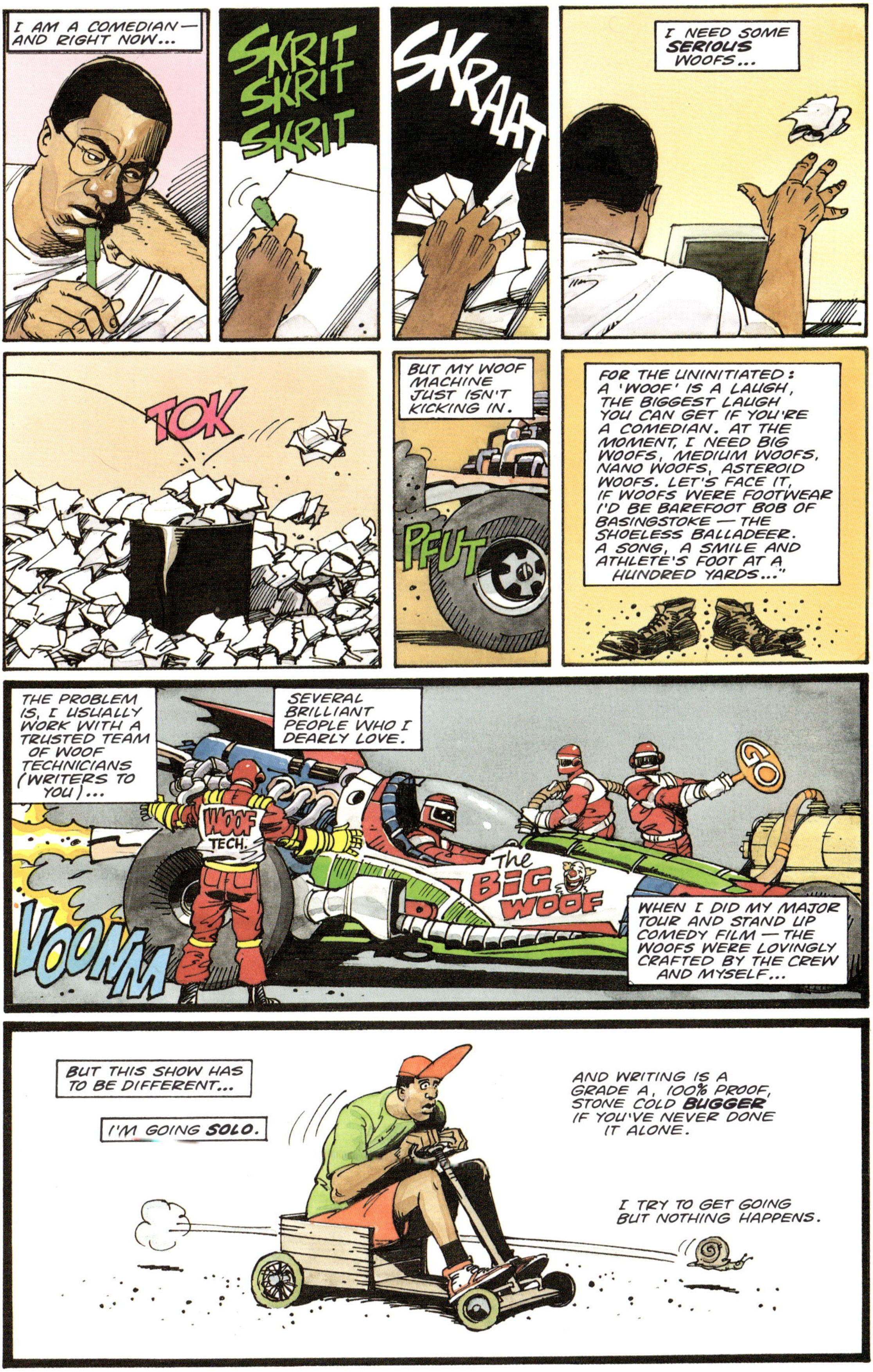

I AM A COMEDIAN— AND RIGHT NOW...
SKRIT SKRIT SKRIT
SKRAAT
I NEED SOME **SERIOUS** WOOFS...
TOK
BUT MY WOOF MACHINE JUST ISN'T KICKING IN.
PFUT
FOR THE UNINITIATED: A 'WOOF' IS A LAUGH, THE BIGGEST LAUGH YOU CAN GET IF YOU'RE A COMEDIAN. AT THE MOMENT, I NEED BIG WOOFS, MEDIUM WOOFS, NANO WOOFS, ASTEROID WOOFS. LET'S FACE IT, IF WOOFS WERE FOOTWEAR I'D BE BAREFOOT BOB OF BASINGSTOKE — THE SHOELESS BALLADEER. A SONG, A SMILE AND ATHLETE'S FOOT AT A HUNDRED YARDS..."
THE PROBLEM IS, I USUALLY WORK WITH A TRUSTED TEAM OF WOOF TECHNICIANS (WRITERS TO YOU)...
SEVERAL BRILLIANT PEOPLE WHO I DEARLY LOVE.
WOOF TECH.
GO
The BIG WOOF
VOONM
WHEN I DID MY MAJOR TOUR AND STAND UP COMEDY FILM — THE WOOFS WERE LOVINGLY CRAFTED BY THE CREW AND MYSELF...
BUT THIS SHOW HAS TO BE DIFFERENT...
I'M GOING **SOLO**.
AND WRITING IS A GRADE A, 100% PROOF, STONE COLD **BUGGER** IF YOU'VE NEVER DONE IT ALONE.
I TRY TO GET GOING BUT NOTHING HAPPENS.

16 TONS
DON'T TELL ME...
16 TONS
CRUNCH
I'M THE FIRST WRITER TO START HIS CAREER WITH A **BLOCK** THE SIZE OF **GODZILLA'S TESTICLES**.
WHATEVER THIS SHOW IS...
IT BETTER BE AS GOOD AS THE LAST ONE...
The New Throwdown
I USED TO GO CLUBBING ALL THE TIME...
WOOF!
UM... PASS THOSE YOUNG LADIES THIS WAY, PLEASE...
IT SEEMS THEY'VE BEEN *OVERCOME* BY *SHEER MERRIMENT*.
EXIT
THIS GEEZER IS A BLOODY GENIUS. AM I RIGHT, BERNARD?
YOU ARE NOT WRONG, BYRON.
YEAH, MAN... THAT WAS A GOOD SHOW...
RIING!

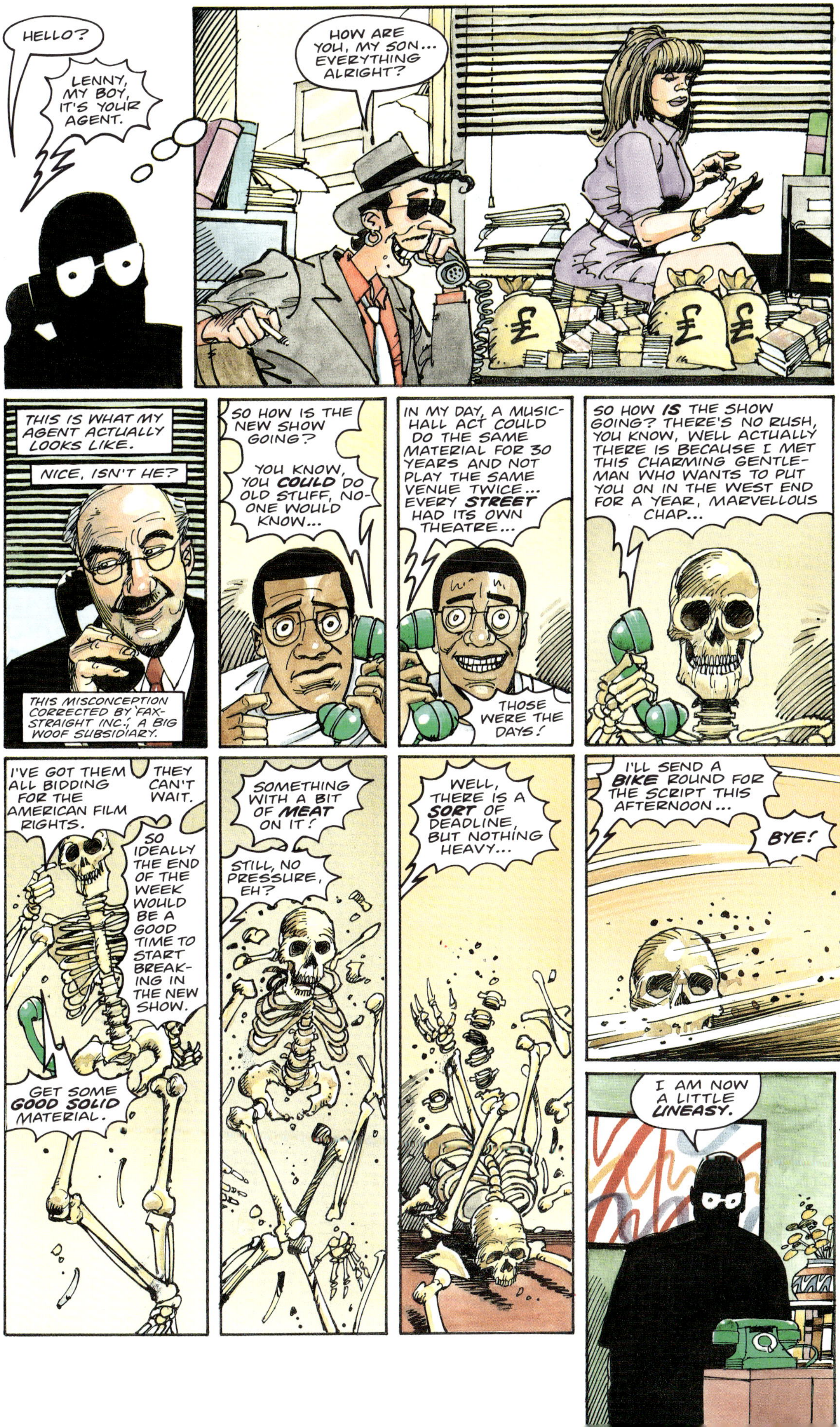
HELLO?
LENNY, MY BOY, IT'S YOUR AGENT.
HOW ARE YOU, MY SON... EVERYTHING ALRIGHT?
THIS IS WHAT MY AGENT ACTUALLY LOOKS LIKE.
NICE, ISN'T HE?
THIS MISCONCEPTION CORRECTED BY 'FAX-STRAIGHT INC.', A BIG WOOF SUBSIDIARY.
SO HOW IS THE NEW SHOW GOING?
YOU KNOW, YOU COULD DO OLD STUFF, NO-ONE WOULD KNOW...
IN MY DAY, A MUSIC-HALL ACT COULD DO THE SAME MATERIAL FOR 30 YEARS AND NOT PLAY THE SAME VENUE TWICE... EVERY STREET HAD ITS OWN THEATRE...
THOSE WERE THE DAYS!
SO HOW IS THE SHOW GOING? THERE'S NO RUSH, YOU KNOW, WELL ACTUALLY THERE IS BECAUSE I MET THIS CHARMING GENTLE-MAN WHO WANTS TO PUT YOU ON IN THE WEST END FOR A YEAR, MARVELLOUS CHAP...
I'VE GOT THEM ALL BIDDING FOR THE AMERICAN FILM RIGHTS.
THEY CAN'T WAIT.
SO IDEALLY THE END OF THE WEEK WOULD BE A GOOD TIME TO START BREAK-ING IN THE NEW SHOW.
GET SOME GOOD SOLID MATERIAL.
SOMETHING WITH A BIT OF MEAT ON IT!
STILL, NO PRESSURE, EH?
WELL, THERE IS A SORT OF DEADLINE, BUT NOTHING HEAVY...
I'LL SEND A BIKE ROUND FOR THE SCRIPT THIS AFTERNOON...
BYE!
I AM NOW A LITTLE UNEASY.

ANCTIONS
AAAAAAA
AARRRGHHHH
HOT PANTS!
AAAOOOW!
JUMP BACK! WANNA KISS MYSELF! HUH!
JAAAAAAMES BROWN! * HEYYYY!
* IN-MODULE ENTERTAINMENT— IT'S THE NEWEST THANG...
-ZZZZZZZZZZZZZ
HONK

Whimper
GRUMBLE
SNORE
uurgh...
DEADLINE!
aargh!
PAD
PAD
PAD
PAD
CLICK
TINKLE
TINKLE
TINKLE
TINKLE
TINKLE
TINKLE
TINKLE
TINKLE
TINKLE
TINKLE
TINKLE
TINKLE
TINKLE
SHAKE
SHAKE
WIPE
WIPE
WIPE...
CLICK
PAD
PAD
PAD
DONK!
OW!
NNN...
Whimper
GRUMBLE
Whine
UH
UH
UH
SSSSSS
?
FLAP
FLAP
!
WHU
WHU
WHU
PFFFT!
?!
POKE
POKE
FUMBLE
CLICK

WOW! IT'S DAWN...†
CRIKEY! SHE IS SOOOOOOO GORGEOUS!
DAWN? WHAT'S GOING ON?
DAWN! SPEAK TO ME!
AUGH!
AAGH!
†DAWN FRENCH IS AVAILABLE FOR ALL TYPES OF WORK, THEATRICAL ENGAGEMENTS, MOVING PICTURE PRODUCTIONS AND PERSONAL APPEARANCES. CALL AGENT FOR DETAILS.
THANKS FOR MAKING ME LOOK SO FAB, STEVE... I'LL GIVE YOU THE PRESENT LATER. DF
OKAY, PUNK— DROP 'EM!
DAWN? WHAT IS IT?
JUST PLAYING WITH THE MEDIUM, LUVVY.
NOW THEN... WHAT'S UP?
YOU'VE BEEN GRUNTING, MOANING, GASPING, SCREAMING, TOSSING AND TURNING...
I WOULDN'T MIND...
...BUT IT'S NOT EVEN THAT NIGHT OF THE WEEK...
SO... WHAT'S THE MATTER?

WELL, I'M JUST WORRIED ABOUT THE NEW SHOW — I'VE BEEN TRYING TO WRITE IT MYSELF, BUT IT'S JUST NOT COMING.
MY AGENT'S BOOKED THE THEATRES...
AND WE START TRYOUTS SOON. I CAN SENSE IT ALL GOING WRONG.
SO... ER... ANYWAY... THE OZONE LAYER... UM... I'M GREEN, Y'KNOW. WELL, WHEN I SAY THAT... ER...
OBVIOUSLY I'M NOT TALKING ABOUT... WELL, YOU KNOW.
LET'S GO AN' 'AVE A DRINK. THIS GUY STINKS.
EXIT
POOOOOWEE!
YOU SEE, I WANTED TO RETAIN THE INTEGRITY OF THE ACT... KEEP IT, YOU KNOW, RELEVANT.
TOUCH UPON SIGNIFICANT ISSUES, REFLECT THE SHIFT IN PUBLIC AWARE...
UH?
ZZZZZZ
HUH!
GIRLIES!

MEANWHILE...
I'VE GOT A SILVER MACHINE!
POIT!
OKAY, OKAY, I'VE READ RAYMOND CHANDLER. I'VE READ WILLIAM GOLDMAN'S 'ADVENTURES IN THE SCREEN TRADE!' I'VE READ 'HOW TO BE GROOVY IN 3 EASY LESSONS' BY ALAN MOORE...
IF YOU WANNA BE A WRITER... YOU'VE GOTTA WRITE!
THEY ALL SAY THE SAME THING.
SO THAT'S IT. I'M JUST GONNA DO IT. THAT'S THE ONLY WAY.
HEY! JEFFREY ARCHER'S A WRITER. THERE'S HOPE!
SANCTIONS NOW
YO!
WAY TO GO!
GAGS
UH...
HUH?
GAGS

GAGS
HELP ME! GOD HELP ME!
BETTER GET A COAT, MAN. IT'S COLD OUT HERE!

MAYBE I'LL USE THE COMPUTER...
TAP TAP TAP
JUST WRITE. THAT'S ALL YOU HAVE TO DO.
TAP TAP TAP TAP
HA! THE OLD JUICE IS BACK!
HEY, THIS IS EASY!
TAP TAP TAP TAP TAP
TAP TAP TAP
TAP TAP TAP TAP
OKAY.
LET'S HAVE A PRINT-OUT.
OH NO!!
All work and no
All work and no play makes Jack a dull boy
All work and no play makes Jack a dull boy
All work and no play makes Jack a dull boy
All work and no play makes Jack a dull boy
All work and no play makes Jack a dull boy
All work and no play makes Jack a dull boy
All work and no play makes Jack a dull boy
All work and no play makes Jack a dull boy
All work and no play makes Jack a dull boy
All work and no play makes Jack a dull boy
All work and no play makes Jack a dull boy
All work and no play makes Jack a dull boy
All work and no play makes Jack a dull boy
All work and no play makes Jack a dull boy
All work and no play makes Jack a dull boy
All work and no play makes Jack a dull boy
All work and no play makes Jack a dull boy
All work and no play makes Jack a dull boy
All work and no play makes Jack a dull boy
All work and no play makes Jack a dull boy
All work and no play makes Jack a dull boy
All work and no play makes Jack a dull boy
All work and no play makes Jack a dull boy
All work and no play makes Jack a dull boy
All work and no play makes Jack a dull boy
All work and no play makes Jack a dull boy
All work and no play makes Jack a dull boy
All work and no play makes Jack a dull boy
All work and no play makes Jack a dull boy
All work and no play makes Jack a dull boy
All work and no play makes Jack a dull boy
All work and no play makes Jack a dull boy
All work and no play makes Jack a dull boy
All work and no play makes Jack a dull boy
All work and no play makes Jack a dull boy
All work and no play makes Jack a dull
All work and no play makes

CABIN FEVER!
UH, OH LENNY, MADJACK ATTACK.*
SANCTIONS NOW
* LENNY HAS SEEN 'THE SHINING' 45 TIMES... SORRY. Ed.
THOK
CRAK
WOK
HEEERE'S LENNY!
NOW
THAK!
DIE, COMPUTER!
JACK NICHOLSON, EAT YOUR HEART OUT!
CRASH
DIE, BOOKS!
DIE, POT PLANT!
CHOK

I DUNNO. MAYBE IF I WAS BETTER EDUCATED.
SANCTIONS NOW
MAYBE THINGS WOULD BE EASIER IF I HAD SOME... QUALIFICATIONS!
TABULA RASA, EMPTY, NADA— Absobloodylutely nil.
"SOME DEGREES AND STUFF ...LIKE EVERYBODY ELSE IN COMEDY SEEMS TO HAVE."
JERRY LEWIS: BA.
BUD ABBOT: DSC.
LOU COSTELLO: Lib. MMSC. (Hons)
JOAN RIVERS: Dip. Ag. BA.
MOMS MABLEY: D.Phil., BA., MBA. (Hons.)
BOB HOPE: Phd. D.Phil.
BILL COSBY: DD., MB., BCher.
TRACEY ULLMAN: DCM and Bar, 2 CSE's.
MEL BROOKS: VC. HNC. MBA. Phd. and VD.
JACK BENNY: HNC. DFC. VC.
"BUT NAAH. I WAS TOO BUSY AT SCHOOL LOOKING OUT THE WINDOW."

LENNY
"HE'S SUCH A BAD PENNY"
PLAYBOY
RIGHT, YOU LOT. TODAY WE'RE DOING HISTORY.
YOU KNOW IF YOU COMBED THAT HAIR OUT YOU COULD HAVE A DECENT AFRO.
I'LL BE TALKING ABOUT ISAMBARD KINGDOM BRUNEL.
LISTEN, YOU COULD HAVE PLASTIC SURGERY
NOBODY SHOULD GO THROUGH LIFE THAT UGLY.
I WONDER IF ANY OF THESE CHILDREN REACH MATURITY. AND WHAT WILL THEY BE LIKE WHEN THEY DO?
"LANCE 'LORD' SNOOTY—CHARGED WITH DRUG-DEALING, GUN RUNNING AND MISLEADING SMALL CHILDREN."
50396123
"MS. P. POTTER, AUTHOR OF AWARD-WINNING BOOK, STRONG MAN'S DAUGHTER, SOCIAL WORKER'S WIFE..."
WAKE UP, BOY!
DONK
OW!

MAYBE I NEED A CUP OF TEA.
YEAH, TEA.
LENMAN in DARK COMIC
TEA KEPT THIS GREAT COUNTRY OF OURS GOING...
DURING THE BIG ONE.
GOT TO... UUH KEEP GOING. GET TO THE UUGHH... SINK...
KEEP TALKING... YEAH... THAT'S IT, OLD SOLDIER...
TEA HAS ENOUGH CAFFEINE TO GIVE ME THE... AHH... KICK OF ADRENALINE...
UUNGHH... TURN ON THE FAUCET...
DON'T SWEAT IT, OLD PAL.
DRIP DRIP DRIP
I'LL MAKE US THIS TEA...
I FORGOT MY BELT!
THERE'S TEA IN THE POUCHES!
ASSAM
LAPSANG SOUCHONG
CAMOMILE
WRITHING IN MY GULLET... THIS THING CALLED THIRST TELLS ME WHAT I NEED...
MAYBE I'LL JUST GIVE IN AND RING THE WOOF POSSE...
YEAH... WHO NEEDS THIS BULLSHIT?
BING BONG
PROBABLY THE SCOUTS OR THE MOONIES. COR, WHAT A LIFE, EH, READERS?

I HEARD YOU NEEDED SOME HELP... WELL YOU COULD AT LEAST HAVE BAKED ME A CAKE.
!
ARE YOU ROOTED TO THE SPOT OR DO YOU ALWAYS SWEAT CHLOROPHYLL?
WELL, ARE YOU GONNA LET ME IN OR WHAT?
MAYBE I'LL JUST CAMP OUT HERE.
HELL, I COULD CAMP OUT ANYWHERE.
OHH, GIVE ME A HOME WHERE THE BUFFALO ROAM...
CAN'T YOU SEE WHAT I'M TRYING TO SAY? I **LOVE** YOU, NO-ONE CAN SAY IT'S WRONG...
SLAM!

BING
SANCTIONS NOW
BONG
I WANNA BE LOVED BY YOU...
JUST YOU...
AND NOBODY ELSE BUT YOU...
IF YOU WANTED ME TO... I COULD HELP YOU WITH YOUR...
LITTLE PROBLEM...
SLAM!
THAT WASN'T MARILYN...
THAT WASN'T GROUCHO.
I'M JUST DAYDREAMING AGAIN.
I'M ALWAYS LIKE THIS...
I WAS LIKE THIS AT WORK, AT SCHOOL...
IT'S A DAYDREAM.
BING BONG

EEEP! YOU KNOW IF YOU DON'T LET ME IN, I MIGHT HAVE TO STAY LIKE THIS FOREVER...
IT COULD LEAD TO INGROWING TOE NAILS...
YA GONNA LET ME IN? OOOH!
NAAH! YOU'RE NOT THE REAL THING...
YOU'RE NOT NEARLY **BONKERS** ENOUGH!
YOU KNOW IF YOU LET ME IN I COULD HELP YOU...
SLAM!
THIS ISN'T HAPPENING.
MY DEAR FELLOW, AT **LAST** I GET TO SEE THE HALLWAY.

H-HOW DID YOU G-G-?
WHERE D-D-DID YOU G-G-GET THAT **COAT?**
THIS OLD THING?
OH, I JUST BORROWED IT FROM A **FRIEND...**
... JOSEPH? YOU MAY HAVE HEARD OF HIM.
WELL, YES. HE HAS GOT SHOPS ALL OVER LONDON... BUT USUALLY IT'S LITTLE BLACK NUMBERS, NOTHING LIKE **THIS!**
UHH... NO. NOT **THAT** JOSEPH.
THINK IN A MORE **HISTORICAL** SENSE...
COME ON, BRAIN! *UNNNNGH...* NO. CAN'T DO IT.
WHO **ARE** YOU?
WELL, I'M THE ALMIGHTY COOL RULER. THE LIGHT. THE WAY. THE TRUTH...
"JOHNNY MIRACLES. THE BIG CHEESE..."
The Buddha!
JAH!
JeHOVAH!
THE BOSS. BASICALLY I'M BLOODY GOD...
WANG
...AND I'M BURSTING FOR A CUP OF TEA!

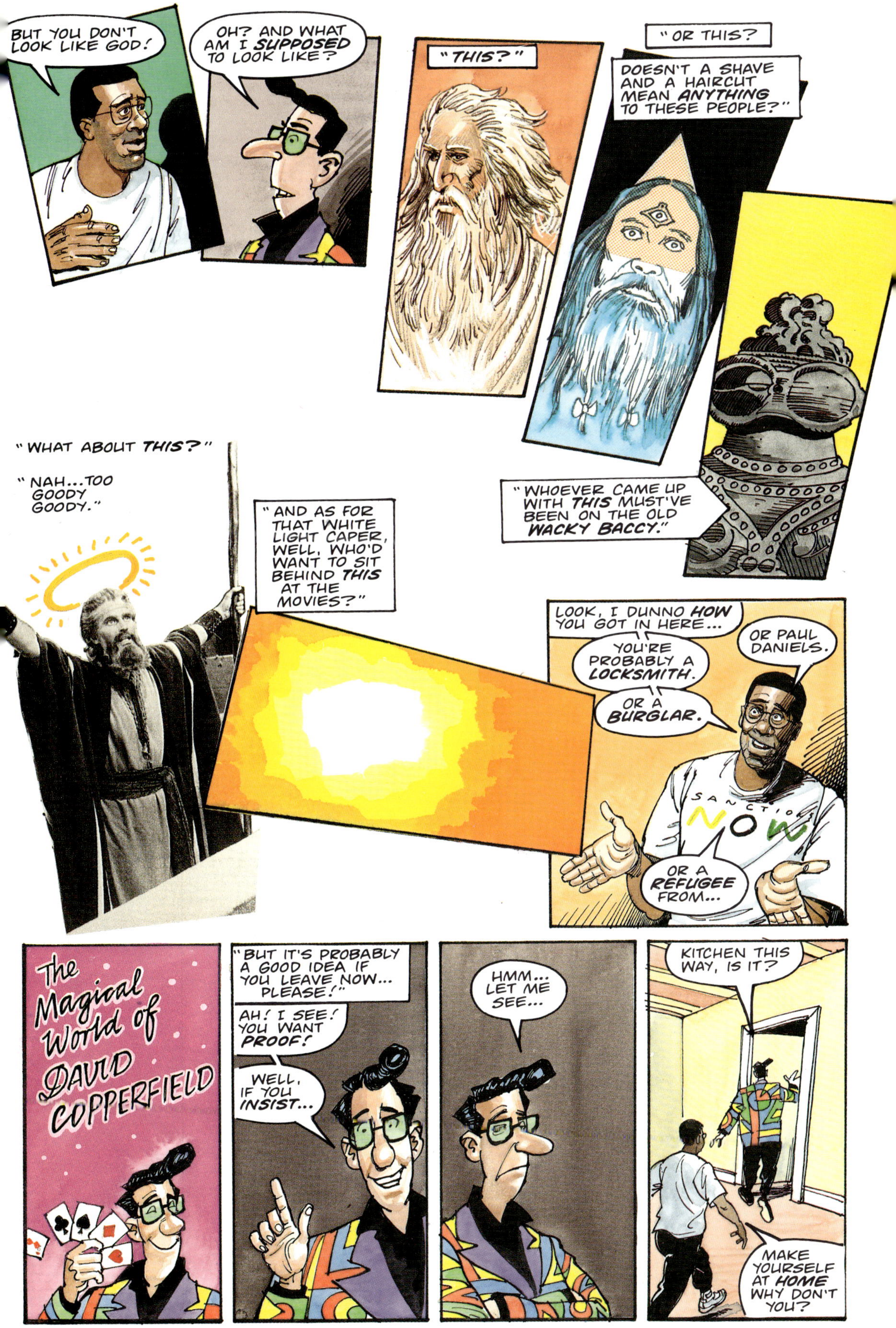

BUT YOU DON'T LOOK LIKE GOD!
OH? AND WHAT AM I SUPPOSED TO LOOK LIKE?
"THIS?"
"OR THIS?
DOESN'T A SHAVE AND A HAIRCUT MEAN ANYTHING TO THESE PEOPLE?"
"WHOEVER CAME UP WITH THIS MUST'VE BEEN ON THE OLD WACKY BACCY."
"WHAT ABOUT THIS?"
"NAH...TOO GOODY GOODY."
"AND AS FOR THAT WHITE LIGHT CAPER, WELL, WHO'D WANT TO SIT BEHIND THIS AT THE MOVIES?"
LOOK, I DUNNO HOW YOU GOT IN HERE...
YOU'RE PROBABLY A LOCKSMITH.
OR A BURGLAR.
OR PAUL DANIELS.
OR A REFUGEE FROM...
SANCTION NOW
The Magical World of DAVID COPPERFIELD
"BUT IT'S PROBABLY A GOOD IDEA IF YOU LEAVE NOW... PLEASE!"
AH! I SEE! YOU WANT PROOF!
WELL, IF YOU INSIST...
HMM... LET ME SEE...
KITCHEN THIS WAY, IS IT?
MAKE YOURSELF AT HOME WHY DON'T YOU?

PILCHARDS IN TOMATO SAUCE
HOLY BUTTOCK HAIR!
WHAT AM I SUPPOSED TO DO... OPEN A FISHULIKE?
MAKE THEM GO AWAY!

I THOUGHT YOU WANTED PROOF?
YES, BUT WHY ALL THIS?
WELL, IT WORKED BEFORE—AND I ALWAYS SAY 'IF AN OLD GAG WORKED ONCE, IT'LL WORK AGAIN!
SANCTIONS NOW
BONG!
SNAP!
YOU REALLY ARE HIM!
YES, I SUPPOSE I AM—FEELS GOOD, TOO!
PLEASE GET RID OF THIS STUFF, OH MIGHTY ONE!
THE CAT'LL HAVE AN ORGASMIC FRENZY—AND WE'LL NEVER BE ABLE TO CLEAN THE WINDOWS!
BOF!
WOW! IT'S ALL GONE!
BRRRIPP!

I NEED TO CALM DOWN!
TCH! YOU COULD DIE OF THIRST HERE!
FLIP ME! THAT'S RIGHT... WOULD YOU LIKE A CUP OF TEA?
A DELIGHTFUL IDEA, MY GOOD FELLOW!
SORRY I DIDN'T BELIEVE YOU.
CAMOMILE.
THAT'S OKAY. MMM, THIS IS NICE.
MUST TAKE SOME BACK HOME.
SO. UM... WHY ARE YOU HERE?
THESE THINGS'LL BE THE DEATH OF ME.
WHY AM I HERE?
WELL, I LIKE TO KEEP AN EYE ON PEOPLE...
...AND I CAN'T BE EVERYWHERE...
BUT I THOUGHT...
BUT YOU'RE SUPPOSED TO BE EVERYWHERE!
BLESS YOU, NO—THAT WAS IN THE OLD DAYS. NOWADAYS I'M MORE CHOOSY WHERE I GO.
THAT WAS BEFORE I HAD A SECRETARY.
OH?
"SINCE NAVALETTE CAME ALONG, LIFE HAS BEEN BLISS. I'VE GOT A PERSONAL ORGANISER AND THE OFFICE IS COMPUTERISED."
YOU? THE MIGHTY CAHUNA... WERE DISORGANISED AND NEEDED A SECRETARY?
OOH, YES... I WAS TERRIBLE!
"I INVENTED DINOSAURS AND COULDN'T REMEMBER WHAT THEY WERE FOR!"
"DO YOU REMEMBER NOW?"
"WELL, I REMEMBER JAMMING IN THE PRIMORDIAL OOZE..."
"AND THESE WEIRD SHAPES KEPT SUGGESTING THEMSELVES TO ME...
SO I WHACKED THE BREATH OF LIFE INTO THEM..."
HAH

"VOILA! NIGHT OF THE LIVING BONEHEADS...
BOY WERE THEY DUMB."
HERE WE GO!
HERE WE GO!
HERE WE GO!
MANCHESTER UNITED
WANNA SEE?
ERRR...
BOOF
NOW
UMM... SO THIS IS LONGLEAT.
RAAAAAH

OH DON'T BE SUCH A BIG BABY!
THIS THING PROBABLY CAN'T EVEN SEE YOU. LET'S TAKE A CLOSER LOOK!

SEE, I SHOULD'VE GIVEN IT A BIGGER BRAIN...
THEN AT LEAST I WOULD'VE HAD SOME COMPANY IN THE EARLY DAYS...
I MEAN, LOOK AT THIS...
"THAT MINISCULE, USELESS LOOKING OBJECT IN THE CORNER IS HIS BRAIN..."
"I MUST'VE BEEN ASLEEP!"
THIS... IS A TRICERATOPS. IT SERVES NO PURPOSE WHATSOEVER.
MAYBE SOME KIND OF PREHISTORIC HATSTAND?
I'LL IGNORE THAT.
"ANYHOW... I HERALDED THE ICE AGE AND WIPED THE SLATE CLEAN."
"AND YOU KNOW, NOT ONE OF THEM TRIED TO ESCAPE."
"THEY DIDN'T THINK TO UPROOT TWO TREES, STRAP 'EM TO THEIR FEET AND SKI CROSS COUNTRY."
"THEY JUST STOOD AROUND GROPING FOR THE DINOSAUR PHRASE FOR: 'BLOODY HELL, ANYONE GOT A CARDIGAN?'"

YOU'RE PRETTY FUNNY...
WELL, AS KING OF ALL KINGS I'M BOUND TO KNOW A FEW GAGS.
MAYBE YOU CAN HELP. I'M TRYING TO WRITE A NEW SHOW—
I KNOW.
AND YOU WANT IT TO MEAN SOME-THING.
RIGHT.
YOU BLOODY COMICS ARE ALL THE SAME NOWADAYS.
WHATEVER HAPPENED TO JUST HAVING A LAUGH?
I USED TO WET MYSELF AT LAUREL AND HARDY...
"YOU DIDN'T GET THEM PONCING AROUND AT BENEFITS FOR 'NICARAGUAN DOLPHINS AGAINST THE POLL TAX'."
BOLLOCKS TO THE POLL TAX!
RIGHT ON!
YEAH, BUT COMEDY HAS TO MEAN SOMETHING DOESN'T IT?
I'M NOT HERE JUST TO CRACK GAGS.
HMM.
SO WHAT DO YOU WANT TO TALK ABOUT IN THIS NEW SHOW?
WELL, EVERYTHING. RACISM, SEXISM, DRUGS, WAR, DEATH, POLITICS...
AND IT MUST BE FUNNY...
AND MAKE A LOT OF POINTS...
YOU DON'T WANT MUCH, DO YOU?
THE TROUBLE IS, ALL MY BEST STUFF IS ABOUT PERSONAL EXPERIENCES...
SANCTIONS NOW
AND AT THE MOMENT I FEEL SO... DRY.
WELL, LITTLE CHAP. LET'S SEE ABOUT GETTING YOU SOAKED TO THE SKIN, SHALL WE?
BOFF!

WHOA!
WHUP!
HEY!
HA!
PAIN
TRUTH
JUST BREATHE AND EVERYTHING WILL BE COOL.
THIS IS YOUR MIND-ZONE. IT'S LIKE THE TWILIGHT ZONE, BUT DIMMER!
RACISM
HA BLOODY HA!
THIS REPRESENTS WHAT'S GOING ON IN YOUR MIND...
I THINK WE'LL GET A PRETTY GOOD IDEA OF WHAT'S HAPPENING BY DIVING INTO THESE GLOBES.
IS THAT WISE?
I HAD A FRIEND WHO REALLY GOT INTO HIMSELF...
HE NEVER CAME OUT!
DON'T WORRY, YOU'RE WITH ME...
BESIDES...
WHAT HARM COULD WE COME TO?
AFTER ALL... THIS IS YOUR MIND.
SLAVERY

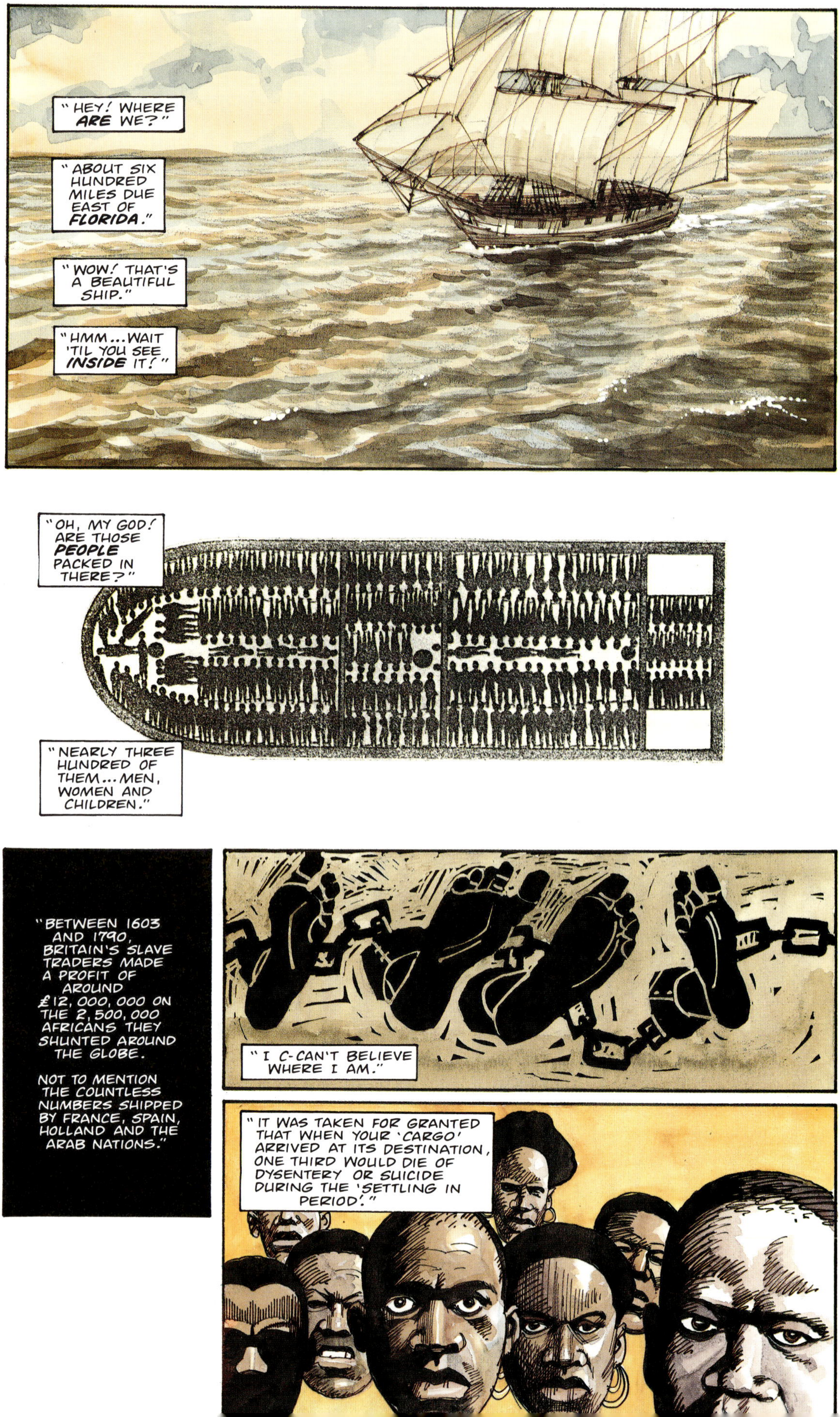
"HEY! WHERE ARE WE?"
"ABOUT SIX HUNDRED MILES DUE EAST OF FLORIDA."
"WOW! THAT'S A BEAUTIFUL SHIP."
"HMM... WAIT 'TIL YOU SEE INSIDE IT!"
"OH, MY GOD! ARE THOSE PEOPLE PACKED IN THERE?"
"NEARLY THREE HUNDRED OF THEM... MEN, WOMEN AND CHILDREN."
"BETWEEN 1603 AND 1790, BRITAIN'S SLAVE TRADERS MADE A PROFIT OF AROUND £12,000,000 ON THE 2,500,000 AFRICANS THEY SHUNTED AROUND THE GLOBE.
NOT TO MENTION THE COUNTLESS NUMBERS SHIPPED BY FRANCE, SPAIN, HOLLAND AND THE ARAB NATIONS."
"I C-CAN'T BELIEVE WHERE I AM."
"IT WAS TAKEN FOR GRANTED THAT WHEN YOUR 'CARGO' ARRIVED AT ITS DESTINATION, ONE THIRD WOULD DIE OF DYSENTERY OR SUICIDE DURING THE 'SETTLING IN PERIOD'."

I READ THAT BOOK. ONE IN THREE AFRICANS DIED DURING THE 3-YEAR SEASONING, OR ACCLIMATIZATION PERIOD.
THIS IS NO BOOK, MY FRIEND. THIS IS THE REAL DEAL... A REAL LIVE SLAVE SHIP!
SHUT UP IN THERE, NEGAR!
WELL... WHAT ARE YOU GONNA DO?
WHAT CAN I DO? I'M A SLAVE! I'M CHAINED UP...
I'M SICK!
I SAID SHUT UP, YOU BLACK DEVIL!
THIS IS BULLSHIT! NO-ONE CALLS ME THAT—NOT SINCE SCHOOL, ANYWAY. HEY, CARBUNCLE FACE, I'M GONNA REPORT YOU!
THIS IS WITCHCRAFT! I NEVER HEARD ONE TALK LIKE THIS BEFORE!
I'D BETTER GET TERRY.
YOU CAN'T TREAT PEOPLE LIKE THIS!
"BLOODY SLAVE TRADE. MOVING MILLIONS OF AFRICANS ALL OVER THE PLACE JUST SO SOME PAMPERED OLD BAT IN A POWDERED WIG GETS TO PUT SUGAR IN HER TEA!"

WHAT'S GOING ON HERE?
WHO'S THE DARKIE WITH THE MAGIC TONGUE, EH?
IT'S ME. AND I'M TELLING YOU NOW... I'M MAKING A CITIZEN'S ARREST!
BLOODY DEVILS!
YOU KEEP THAT WHIP TO YOURSELF!
YEAH. MY FRIENDS AT AMNESTY WILL GET A FULL REPORT!
AMNESTY??
WHY, YOU BLACK IMP, I'LL—
BOF!
WHAT WOULD YOU LIKE TO HAPPEN NOW, MY FRIEND?
YOU MEAN, I CAN DECIDE?
OF COURSE! IT'S A GRAPHIC NOVEL, REMEMBER?
WELL, I'D LIKE TO SEE THESE GUYS SET FREE.
AND MAYBE SEE SOME BUTT KICKED.
IT SHALL BE DONE!
FIRST THE MANACLES...
BOF!
THEN ADD A FEW SPECIAL EFFECTS!

CAP'N! THE SLAVES ARE ESCAPING!
DON'T FRET, MISTER BO'SUN! WE'RE READY AND WAITING!
LET'S BE CHARITABLE, GENTLEMEN... SET YOUR WEAPONS ONE INCH FROM DEATH!
THANKS, MAN... YOU'RE MY HOMEBOY!
YOU HEARD HIM!
LET'S KICK SOME ASS... THEN FIGURE OUT HOW TO GET THIS THING BACK TO THE GAMBIA!
BOF

WOW! I WISH IT COULD'VE BEEN LIKE THAT! THOSE BASTARDS HAD IT COMING!
YES... BUT THESE THINGS CAN BE TURNED AROUND...
EVENTUALLY...
...LIKE ALL OPPRESSION CAN...
WATER CAN ERODE THE HARDEST ROCK...
A TINY FLOWER CAN SPLIT A PAVING STONE...
WHAT GOES AROUND... COMES AROUND.
COME ON! PLACES TO GO! PEOPLE TO SEE!
JUNGLE NUTS
AHH... I KNOW WHERE WE ARE. THIS IS THE MOTHERLAND...
AFRICA!
YES. THIS IS THE FIRST PLACE I HAD A GO AT...
I DID MY BEST WORK FIRST...
LIKE ORSON WELLES.
I'M PARTICULARLY PROUD OF THESE GUYS.
I COULD USE A GOOD WALLOW MYSELF!
IT'S SWELTERING HERE.
OW! I'VE SUDDENLY GOT TERRIBLE TOOTHACHE!
AHH! THIS REALLY HURTS!
NOW I KNOW HOW THE OSMOND BROTHERS FELT!
"I JUST THOUGHT YOU'D LIKE TO BE IN A MORE APPROPRIATE FORM."

THIS IS AMAZING! IN A CERTAIN LIGHT I LOOK LIKE JOHN HURT!
HELLO, MY BROTHERS! MAY YOUR TRUNKS NEVER BE BLOCKED!
I'M GEORGE... AND YOU ARE...?
ER... HE'S MANILOW AND I'M ELVIS.
WELL, MANNY, ELVIS... LET'S DO THAT THING THAT WE ELEPHANTS LOVE TO DO?
WHAT'S THAT? I'VE FORGOTTEN!
HA! HA! AN ELEPHANT THAT FORGETS, THAT'S A GOOD ONE!
NO, MY BROTHER, WE MUST SIT AND REMINISCE ABOUT DROPPINGS.
COME.
"GENTLE READER, NEEDLESS TO SAY, ELEPHANTS DISCUSSING THE SIZE OF THEIR TURDS IS NOT FOR HUMAN EARS.
SUFFICE TO SAY, A PLEASANT AFTERNOON WAS SPENT ROLLING, SPLASHING, AND RAPPING ABOUT POO."
"UNTIL..."
CAN YOU HEAR SOMETHING?
ARE YOU KIDDING?
WITH THESE EARS I COULD HEAR A GNAT CRAP IN LEEDS.
VROOM!
SOUNDS LIKE ENGINES!
WE'VE GOT UNWELCOME GUESTS... RUN!
WHAT DO THEY WANT?
GUESS!

CAN'T YOU DO SOMETHING?
NO FINGERS!
...I CAN'T DO THE MAGICAL GESTURE!
CRAK
THEY'VE GOT GEORGE!
OH SHIT!
VROMM
UUUH

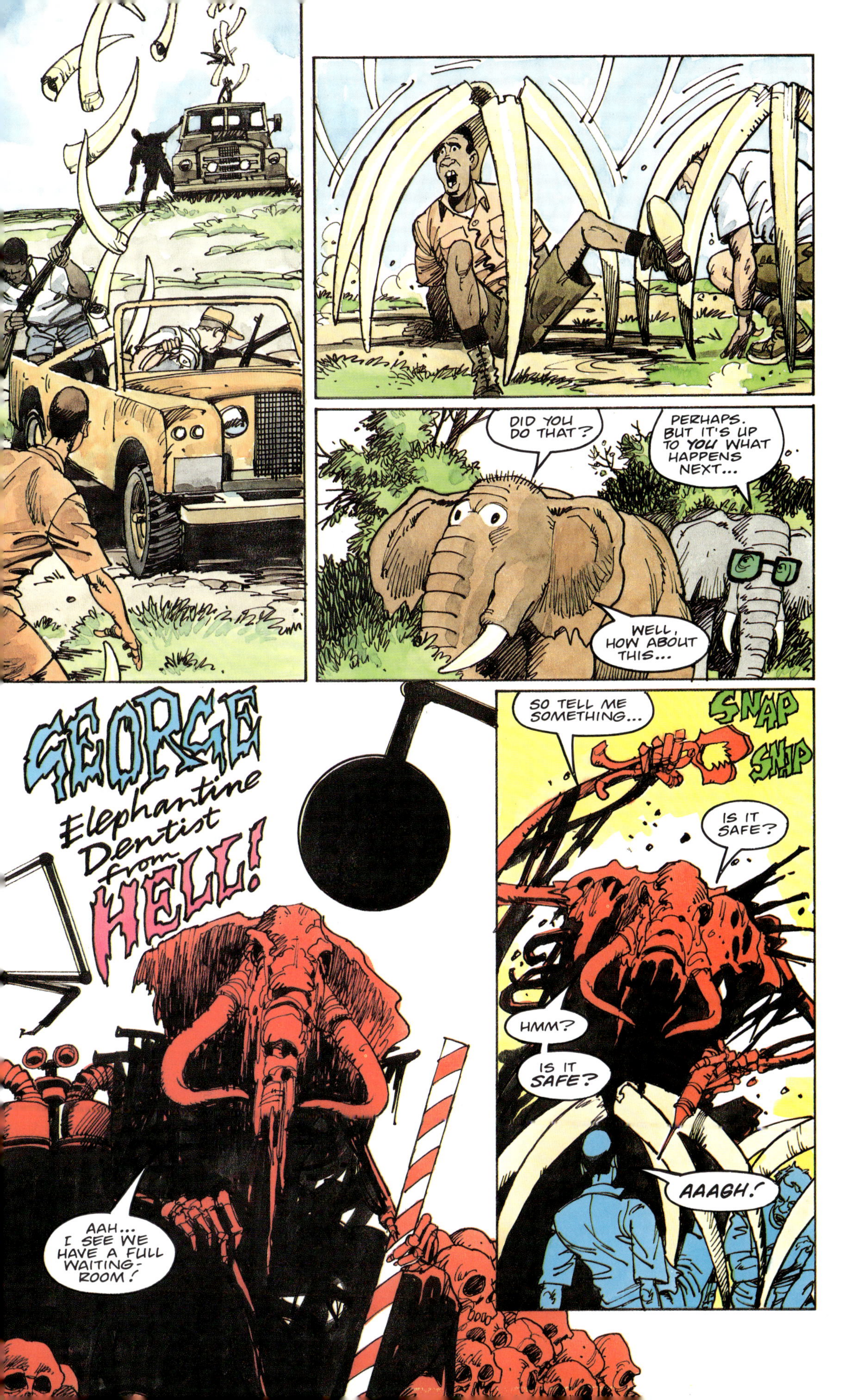
DID YOU DO THAT?
PERHAPS. BUT IT'S UP TO YOU WHAT HAPPENS NEXT...
WELL, HOW ABOUT THIS...
GEORGE
Elephantine Dentist from HELL!
AAH... I SEE WE HAVE A FULL WAITING-ROOM!
SO TELL ME SOMETHING...
SNAP
SNIP
IS IT SAFE?
HMM?
IS IT SAFE?
AAAGH!

WELL, IT MIGHT MAKE THEM LAUGH.
I DUNNO. I CAN'T SOLVE THE ELEPHANT PROBLEM.
YOU'RE GOD.
YOU DO SOMETHING!
YOU MEAN, HELP THE WIDDLE BABIES WIPE DERE WIDDLE BOTTOMS?
WELL... YEAH.
"LOOK... I LOVE YOU PEOPLE. ALWAYS WILL. I WAS SO PROUD OF YOU IN THE BEGINNING...
MY BABY.
"WHEN YOU TOOK YOUR FIRST STEP."
"DISCOVERED FIRE..."
YEOW!
"AND THE WHEEL..."
UUURK!
"BUT THEN YOU SPRANG A FEW SURPRISES..."
COVET
COVET
"EVERY COMMANDMENT THAT COULD BE BROKEN, WAS BROKEN...
MURDER MURDER
NEIGHBOUR'S WIFE
MAN NEXT DOOR
NEIGHBOUR'S ASS
NEIGHBOUR'S OX
NEIGHBOUR'S VEG
LUST
LUST
"THINGS GOT OUT OF HAND."
"AND I WOULD GO BONKERS AND SMITE EVERYTHING THAT MOVED. MY MOTTO WAS: 'IF IT MOVES, SMITE THE BASTARD."
'THEN I REALISED THAT NATURE AND MANKIND WOULD TAKE CARE OF THEMSELVES. IT WAS MY NEW ROLE TO INSPIRE PEOPLE TO REALISE THEIR FULL POTENTIAL".
"LIKE THIS CHAP."
HE LOOKS FAIRLY ORDINARY. WHAT DID HE DO? INVENT A NEW KIND OF CHOW MEIN?
NO. HE WALKED INTO THE MIDDLE OF A BUSY ROAD AND INSPIRED MILLIONS!
SOME GUY GETS KNOCKED DOWN AND THE WORLD IS INDEBTED? TAKE A REALITY PILL, GUY!
NOW
I DON'T THINK YOU UNDERSTAND.
"LET ME PUT YOU IN THE PICTURE."

大 不
更
取
"OH, YOU MEAN HIM...
"YEAH, I REMEMBER HIM..."

HE WAS BRILLIANT, THEY SAY HE'S DEAD NOW, BUT HE MADE PEOPLE REALISE THAT ONE PERSON CAN MAKE A DIFFERENCE.
SORRY ABOUT THE JOKES.
THAT'S ALRIGHT, ONCE YOU WERE IN THE PICTURE, YOU UNDERSTOOD WHAT WAS GOING ON.
I MUST CAUTION YOU, THOUGH...
IN OUR SEARCH FOR THE REAL WOOF, WE MUST BE AWARE THAT TRUTH, INSPIRATION AND PAIN ARE FACTORS, TOO.
THE BEST WOOFS HIDE GREAT PAIN AND ACT AS CATHARSIS...
AND SOME WOOFS REALLY DO BITE!
INSPIRATION
PAIN
LET'S GO!
WHERE TO?
"BACK TO THE BEGINNING WOULD BE A NIFTY IDEA..."
I KNOW THIS PLACE...
THIS IS WHERE I USED TO LIVE!

A SPIKY GATE AND A BATMAN CAPE... PROVE TO LENNY THERE'S NO ESCAPE!
LITTLE LEN
HE'S TURNED UP AGAIN!
"THERE I AM... GOING TO MY BEST FRIEND'S HOUSE."
"WE WERE REALLY CLOSE...
GREW UP TOGETHER."
DONALD, ARE YOU COMING OUT TO PLAY?
4
I'M NOT GOING TO PLAY WITH YOU... YOU'RE A BLACKIE!
NO, I'M NOT!
YES YOU ARE! MY DAD SAYS!
WELL, IF I'M A BLACKIE ...THEN YOU ARE AS WELL!
GOOD LOGIC, KID.
COME ON! LET'S GO AND PLAY IN THE SANDPIT!
DONALD?
PTUI
HE WAS MY BEST FRIEND ...WE DID EVERYTHING TOGETHER...
...PLAYED WITH EACH OTHER...
...MEASURED EACH OTHER'S WEDDING TACKLE.
WE ATE SUGAR SANDWICHES TOGETHER AND HE DOES THAT!
COME ON! YOU WERE ONLY SEVEN!
I WASN'T EXPECTING TO BE GOBBED AT. WE WERE FRIENDS AGAIN NEXT DAY.
KIDS ARE VERY RESILIENT. THIS IS YOU A BIT LATER.

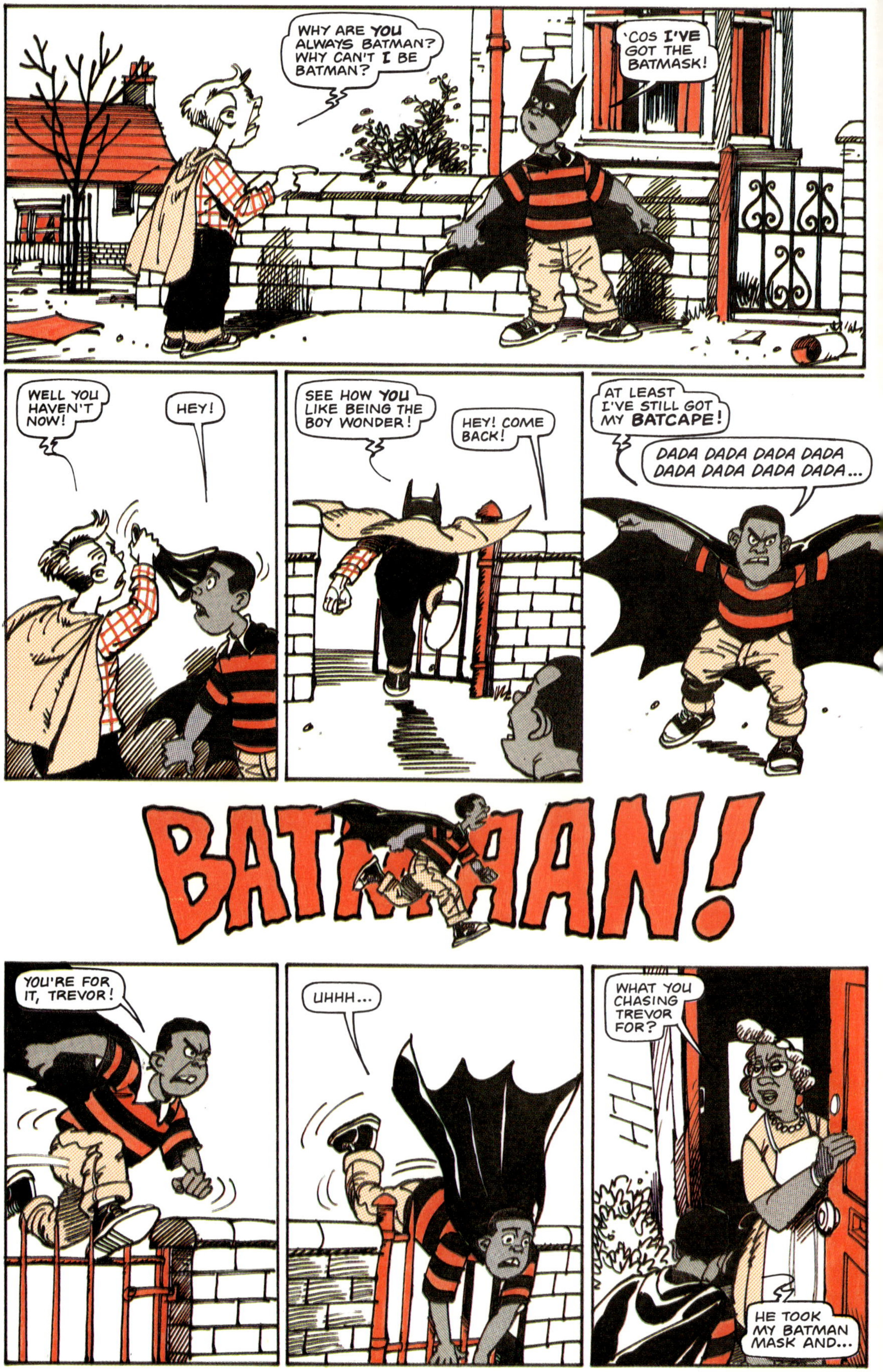
WHY ARE YOU ALWAYS BATMAN? WHY CAN'T I BE BATMAN?
'COS I'VE GOT THE BATMASK!
WELL YOU HAVEN'T NOW!
HEY!
SEE HOW YOU LIKE BEING THE BOY WONDER!
HEY! COME BACK!
AT LEAST I'VE STILL GOT MY BATCAPE!
DADA DADA DADA DADA DADA DADA DADA DADA...
BATMAAN!
YOU'RE FOR IT, TREVOR!
UHHH...
WHAT YOU CHASING TREVOR FOR?
HE TOOK MY BATMAN MASK AND...

LEN... WHAT IS IT?
"OH YEH. IT WAS THEN I SAW THE BLOOD."
AAAGH!
AAGH!
AAAAGH!
AAAAGH!
WOW. THAT WAS HIGH— AT LEAST TOP C.
YEAH, MAN. ISN'T IT WEIRD WHEN YOU'RE A KID?
YOU DON'T FREAK OUT UNTIL YOU SEE YOUR OWN BLOOD.
"SUDDENLY THE CAPE AND MASK WEREN'T SO IMPORTANT. IT WAS LIKE BEING IN VIETNAM..."
MEDIC!
GET MY SON A MEDIC!
DOES THIS GIVE YOU ANY THOUGHTS?
OH YES. I'VE HAD THESE MEMORIES BEFORE, BUT SEEING THEM LIKE THIS MAKES 'EM SEEM MORE REAL.
SOME OF THEM ARE JUST NICE, FUNNY MEMORIES.
OTHERS ARE JUST...
...PAINFUL.
ONWARDS AND UPWARDS.
ANCTIO

LOONY LEN
HE'S AT IT AGAIN!
THAT EMPTY BOX WOULD MAKE A GREAT GARAGE!
HEY, TREV... LOOK WHAT I'VE GOT! LET'S GET OUR CARS AND HAVE A GAME!
RIGHT YOU ARE, LEN!
UH, OH! WHAT'S THAT COMING UP BEHIND? LOOKS LIKE TROUBLE!
THERE IT IS! I NEED THAT BOX!
LEN, DID YOU TAKE THAT BOX FROM THE MAN'S TRUCK?
UM... YES.
GET INDOORS!
OW!
SLAM
"WAS THAT A 'GRADE A' SPANKING?"
"A, B, C, D, E TO INFINITY. I THINK MOM WAS ANGRY BECAUSE SHE WAS SO EMBARRASSED. THE VAN DRIVER PROBABLY WENT BACK TO THE SHOP AND SAID 'THE DARKIES' KID LIFTED SOMETHING OUT OF MY VAN. ANOTHER COUPLE OF YEARS AND HE'LL KNOW HOW TO HOTWIRE THE BLOODY THING!
THAT'S THE KIND OF THING PEOPLE SAID... AND STILL DO. AND IT WAS JUST AN EMPTY BOX!"

"I GOT A BEATING THAT DAY. WEST INDIAN PARENTS TALK TO YOU WHILE YOU'RE GETTING BEATEN, IT'S BETTER THAN HYPNOTISM.
THE WEST INDIAN THEORY: BEAT THE CHILD AND TEACH HIM AT THE SAME TIME.
IF EINSTEIN HAD BEEN JAMAICAN HE WOULD'VE BEEN THREE TIMES AS CLEVER, BUT COMATOSE THROUGH BEING BEATEN SO OFTEN."
DIDN'T I TELL YOU, E=MC²?
I HATED BEING PUNISHED.
I USED TO SAY IF GOD HAD MEANT US TO BE BEATEN... WE WOULD'VE BEEN BORN WITH PADDING.
INTERESTING. ARE YOU PUTTING WORDS IN MY MOUTH?
WELL, I DIDN'T KNOW YOU THEN.
OF COURSE NOT. BUT NOW LET US BE AWAY...
BY THE WAY...
WHAT EXPERIENCE DO YOU HAVE OF DRUGS?
NOW
SANCTION NOW
"WELL, I REMEMBER BEING OVER THE PARK WITH SOME FRIENDS... AND ONE OF THEM SAID HIS BROTHER WAS A HELL'S ANGEL. NONE OF US HAD EVER SEEN A REAL HELL'S ANGEL. EXCEPT ON THE FRONT COVER OF 'CHOPPER' OR 'FREEWHEELIN' FRANK'."
SO WHAT'S THIS SURPRISE THEN, PUD?
MY BROTHER'S GOT SOME TABS, MAN.

WHAT, YOU MEAN LIKE ECZEMA?
NAAH! TABS ISN'T A SKIN DISEASE. IT'S DRUGS. YOU KNOW...
LIKE MARRYJUWANA.
MARRY JOANNA?
WHY SHOULD I MARRY JOANNA, WHOEVER SHE IS?
YOW'M SOFT YOW AM! I MEAN DRUGS! LIKE JIMI HENDRIX AND ALL THEM USED TO TAKE! THEY ALL DROP ACID YOU KNOW.
SO WHEN'S HE GONNA SHOW UP?
I'VE GOT ME HOMEWORK TO DO!
ARE YOU A SISSY OR WHAT? WE'VE GOT A CHANCE TO DO SOME DRUGS AND YOU'RE WORRIED ABOUT HOMEWORK?
ALRIGHT. I'LL WAIT.
I'M NOT A SISSY.
I PLAY FOOTBALL.
I'M OFF HOME, THEN.
ALRIGHT.

THE BLOKE NEVER SHOWED UP. WE WERE THERE FOR SEVEN HOURS!
I BET I WOULD'VE TRIED IT TOO... I WAS SO EASILY LED.
YES. QUITE. TIME TO JET, I THINK.
CLICK
WHAT ARE WE DOING HERE?
I CAN COME TO GLASGOW ANYTIME.
WELCOME TO
GLASGOW
I JUST THOUGHT YOU MIGHT WANT TO SEE A FRIEND OF MINE.
CLICK!
BRIAN... IT'S ME... TERRY.
SEPT 12 1991
UHHH...
OH AYE... SO WHAT YA SAYIN', BIG MAN? GOT ANY TOOLS?
SORRY?
HE MEANS, DO YOU HAVE ANY WORKS, YOU KNOW—FOR SHOOTING UP.
UH, NO... I DON'T HAVE ANY ER... TOOLS.
WELL, THAT'S NO BLUIDY GUID, ES IT?
AH'M SWEATIN' HERE...

I'LL JUST HAVE TAE USE THIS OLD CRAP.
YEAH. I'VE GOT A FEW TOMAZAPAN.
30 OR 40 O' THESE AN' I'LL BE SO FAR OUTTA MA BOX I'LL BE INVESABLE.
HEY—D'YA WANT SOME, PAL? GO AWN, DIP YER BREAD.
WELL... NO THANKS.
I DON'T EVEN SMOKE ACTUALLY.
HEY, TERRY! WHO THE FUCK ES THES?
JULIE ANDREWS?
HNNNN! AHHHHH! GOD HELP ME!
OKAY OKAY.
DON'T WORRY...
YOU'RE OKAY.
I KNOW I'M OKAY, YA BEG JESSIE—I'VE JUST GOT TAE GET SOME DECENT SHIT.
AAAH. THAT FEELS GUID.
SEPT
12
1991
JUNE
JULY
2
AUGUS
SEP
12
1991

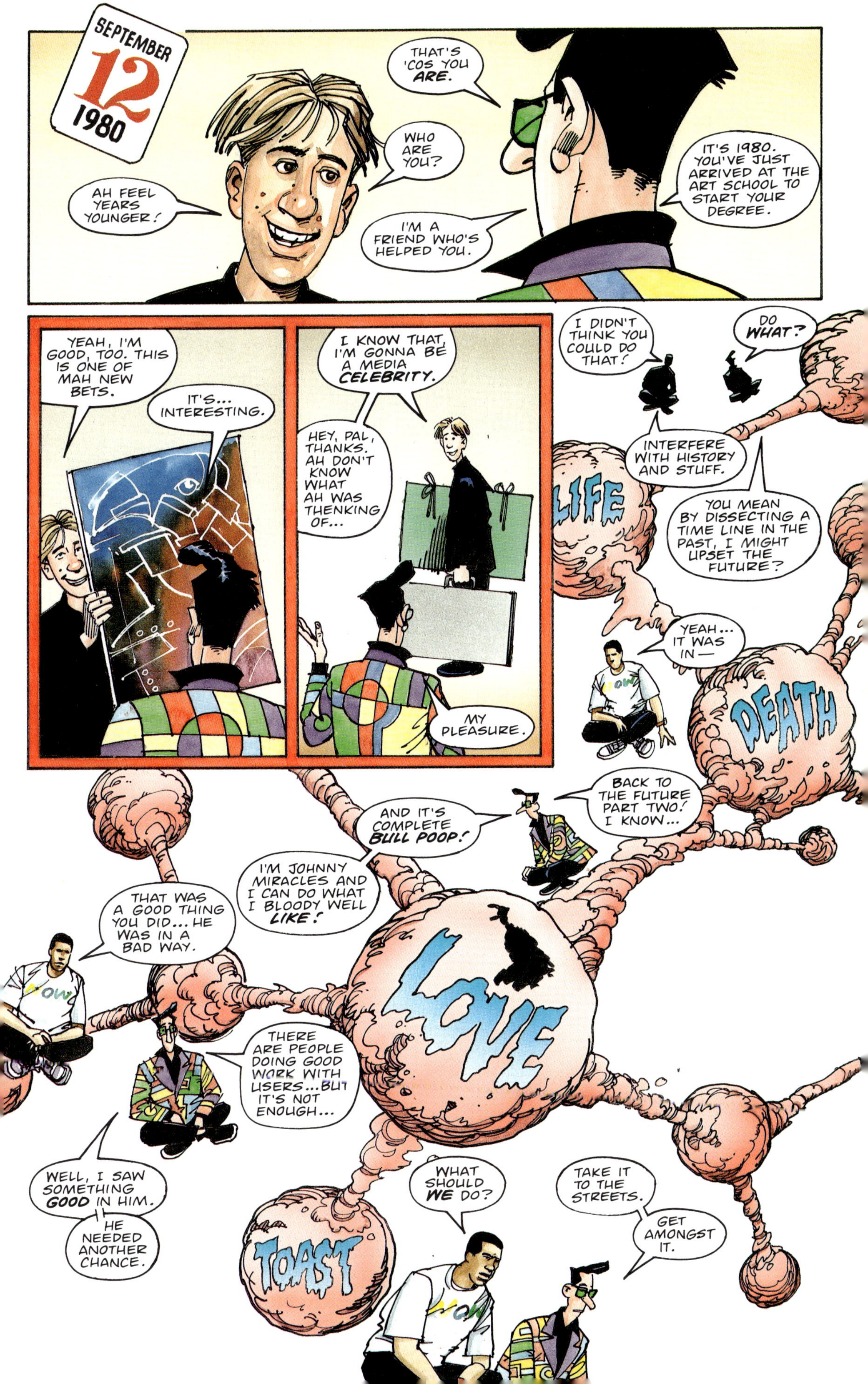
SEPTEMBER 12 1980
AH FEEL YEARS YOUNGER!
THAT'S 'COS YOU ARE.
WHO ARE YOU?
I'M A FRIEND WHO'S HELPED YOU.
IT'S 1980. YOU'VE JUST ARRIVED AT THE ART SCHOOL TO START YOUR DEGREE.
YEAH, I'M GOOD, TOO. THIS IS ONE OF MAH NEW BETS.
IT'S... INTERESTING.
I KNOW THAT. I'M GONNA BE A MEDIA CELEBRITY.
HEY, PAL, THANKS. AH DON'T KNOW WHAT AH WAS THENKING OF...
MY PLEASURE.
I DIDN'T THINK YOU COULD DO THAT!
DO WHAT?
INTERFERE WITH HISTORY AND STUFF.
YOU MEAN BY DISSECTING A TIME LINE IN THE PAST, I MIGHT UPSET THE FUTURE?
LIFE
YEAH... IT WAS IN—
DEATH
BACK TO THE FUTURE PART TWO! I KNOW...
AND IT'S COMPLETE BULL POOP!
I'M JOHNNY MIRACLES AND I CAN DO WHAT I BLOODY WELL LIKE!
THAT WAS A GOOD THING YOU DID... HE WAS IN A BAD WAY.
LOVE
THERE ARE PEOPLE DOING GOOD WORK WITH USERS... BUT IT'S NOT ENOUGH...
WELL, I SAW SOMETHING GOOD IN HIM.
HE NEEDED ANOTHER CHANCE.
WHAT SHOULD WE DO?
TAKE IT TO THE STREETS.
GET AMONGST IT.
TOAST

" I'VE JUST REMEMBERED SOMETHING...
I WAS AT COLLEGE, AND THIS GUY WAS GIVING ME GRIEF... STUPID, RACIST STUFF...
MY FRIENDS KEPT ENCOURAGING ME TO HAVE A GO AT HIM..."
BIG LEN
GO ON, LEN...
SMACK 'IM ONE...
YEAH... CHOP 'IM INA RAAS...
I DON'T WANNA. HE HASN'T DONE ANYTHING WRONG.
THEN...
WHO PUT MY FLAME OUT, HENRY, YOU BLACK BASTARD...
"SOMETHING ROSE UP IN ME FROM 100 MILES AWAY..."
" I COULDN'T HELP MYSELF..."
WAK

"I WAS SO FRIGHTENED. I THOUGHT I'D KILLED THE GUY..."
"...AND I COULDN'T GET MY HAND IN MY POCKET FOR THE NEXT SIX WEEKS..."
THROB
I NEVER WANTED TO FIGHT ANYONE AFTER THAT...
I WAS SICKENED BY THE FEELING OF IT.
"I JUST REALISED IT MIGHT BE POSSIBLE TO LIVE WITHOUT BEING GOADED INTO DOING SOMETHING THAT YOU DIDN'T WANT TO DO...
AM I TALKING OUT OF MY BEHIND?"
"I FEEL LIKE JOHN BOY WALTON..."
WELL, IF YOU'RE VERY GOOD, ELLY-ANNE...
I'LL TELL YOU EXACTLY WHO BUNNY WAILER IS.
YOU KNOW, I'M GETTING A THEME HERE...
MEMORIES FROM MY PAST...
AND EVENTS FROM BLACK HISTORY THAT INSPIRE ME...
IT SEEMS TO BE FULL OF POSSIBILITIES.
I ALWAYS WANTED TO SEE ONE OF THE GREAT MARCHES THAT MARTIN LUTHER KING DID...
YEAH. HE WAS ALRIGHT.
LET'S DO IT! AND REMEMBER... PAIN COUNTS AS INSPIRATION...
CIVIL RIGHTS

MARCHES
EQUAL RIGHTS
EQUAL OPPORTUNITY
NO!
IT'S OKAY. DON'T BE AFRAID.
YOU CAN STAND UP. NOBODY'S GONNA HURT YOU.
I WAS GONNA DO THAT!
WOW!
WOW!
YES. ANY OTHER MINDBLOWING COMMENTS, THEORIES OR PERSPECTIVES ON THAT LAST LITTLE JOURNEY?
WOW!!
WOW
APART FROM "WOW!" ALTHOUGH CONCISE, I DON'T THINK IT WILL DO SOMEHOW.

"THE PEOPLE WHO MARCHED WITH THE CIVIL RIGHTS MOVEMENT WERE SO BRAVE...
I CAN'T REALLY IMAGINE WESTERN PEOPLE DOING NON-VIOLENT PROTESTS THESE DAYS..."
LOOK, YOU CAN'T REALLY CLUB ME SENSELESS TODAY, I'VE GOT A MEETING AT TWO... SO THAT'LL TIE ME UP FOR A WHILE...
AS FOR THE PRESSURE HOSE, WELL, THIS SUIT IS AN ARMANI AND IT'S, LIKE, DRY CLEAN ONLY...
HEY, GIVE ME A COUPLE OF WEEKS, I'LL FIND A 'LUNCH WINDOW' AND WE'LL INTERFACE LIKE CRAZY!
CIAO!
OKAY, WE'RE TRADING STUFF, ... THAT'S GOOD...
REMEMBER, PAIN + INSPIRATION = THE BIG WOOF.
OKAY... WHAT NEXT?
THIS!
S.AFRICA
THIS IS SOUTH AFRICA...
AND THIS IS AFRIKAANS.
I DIDN'T THINK IT UP. TOO MANY K'S AND J'S FOR MY LIKING.
SUMWARE KNEER SOWETO JÜ AH NAH ENJTERING AN (ALMOST) APARTHEID FREE ZONE
THE FAR RIGHT IN THIS COUNTRY SAY THAT APARTHEID IS GOD'S WILL.
I DIDN'T SAY THAT SHIT.
AFRICA IS FOR AFRICANS.

"THEY MADE THAT STUFF UP TO GET ALL THE GOLD AND DIAMONDS."
"THE INDIGENOUS POPULATION DIDN'T KNOW WHAT HIT THEM."
STILL... CHANGE IS COMING.
YEAH. NELSON'S DOING A GREAT JOB.
YOU'D KNOW THIS. WHY WAS HE LATE COMING OUT?
WHAT?
WHY WAS MANDELA LATE LEAVING PRISON? HE WAS AN HOUR LATE.
WELL, HE WANTED TO LOOK AS COOL AS HE COULD.
HE *IS* AFRICAN ROYALTY. HE WANTED THE FUNKIEST CLOTHES AVAILABLE.
"AFTER 27 YEARS IN PRISON...
HE COULD'VE MADE A **SERIOUS** FASHION FAUX PAS!"
WHERE'S YOUR **PASS**, KAFFIR?
SORRY?
YOUR **PASS**.
I DON'T **NEED** ONE!
THWA
DON'T ANSWER BACK, KAFFIR!
OW!
YOU CAN'T DO THIS!
THIS IS **ILLEGAL**!
YOU SHOULDN'T HIT MY FRIEND!
WHO DO YOU THINK YOU ARE NIGGER?
THE BLOODY **POPE**?
NO. I SPEAK ON BEHALF OF A NATION WHO HAVE HAD ENOUGH OF YOUR KIND'S **EVIL**!

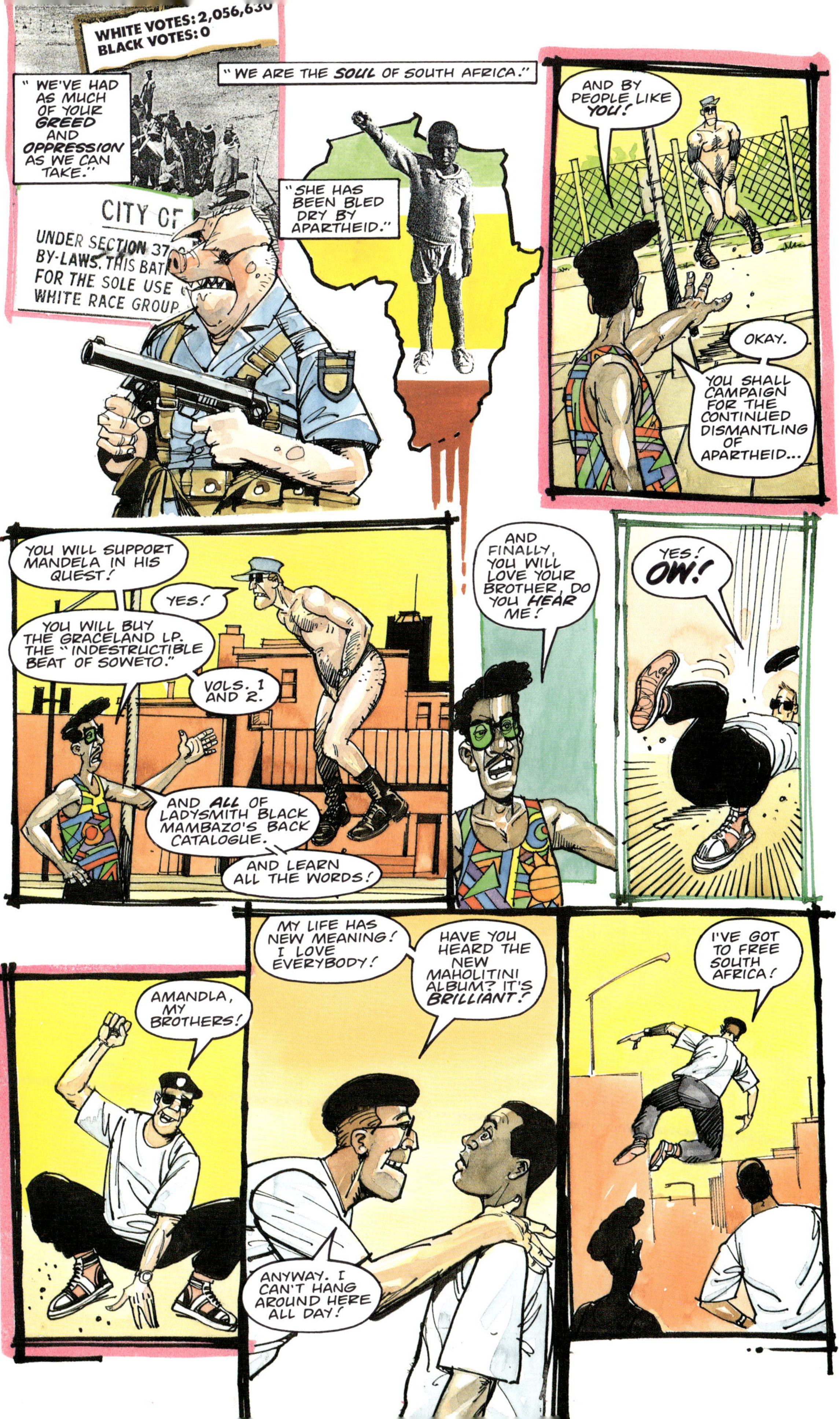

WHITE VOTES: 2,056,630
BLACK VOTES: 0
"WE'VE HAD AS MUCH OF YOUR GREED AND OPPRESSION AS WE CAN TAKE."
CITY OF
UNDER SECTION 37
BY-LAWS. THIS BAT
FOR THE SOLE USE
WHITE RACE GROUP
"WE ARE THE SOUL OF SOUTH AFRICA."
"SHE HAS BEEN BLED DRY BY APARTHEID."
AND BY PEOPLE LIKE YOU!
OKAY.
YOU SHALL CAMPAIGN FOR THE CONTINUED DISMANTLING OF APARTHEID...
YOU WILL SUPPORT MANDELA IN HIS QUEST!
YES!
YOU WILL BUY THE GRACELAND LP. THE "INDESTRUCTIBLE BEAT OF SOWETO."
VOLS. 1 AND 2.
AND ALL OF LADYSMITH BLACK MAMBAZO'S BACK CATALOGUE.
AND LEARN ALL THE WORDS!
AND FINALLY, YOU WILL LOVE YOUR BROTHER, DO YOU HEAR ME!
YES! OW!
AMANDLA, MY BROTHERS!
MY LIFE HAS NEW MEANING! I LOVE EVERYBODY!
HAVE YOU HEARD THE NEW MAHOLITINI ALBUM? IT'S BRILLIANT!
ANYWAY. I CAN'T HANG AROUND HERE ALL DAY!
I'VE GOT TO FREE SOUTH AFRICA!

THAT WAS RADICAL. CAN'T YOU DO THAT FOR THE WHOLE COUNTRY?
NO. THEY MUST FIND THE RIGHT WAY THEMSELVES.
AND THEY WILL... EVENTUALLY.
I HOPE IT'S NOT TOO LONG. I THOUGHT MANDELA WOULD BE IN JAIL 'TIL HE WAS PRUNE-SIZED.
SO HOW DO YOU FEEL NOW?
"WEIRD. LIKE ALL THESE EXPERIENCES WERE THERE TO BE TOUCHED. BUT I WAS TOO LAZY TO REACH OUT."
"LIKE WHAT?"
"LIKE THE TIME I WAS IN UGANDA ON A FARM SPONSORED BY BRITISH COMIC RELIEF. I MET THIS GUY WHO'D BEEN SO BADLY BURNED HIS FACE WAS KINDA WELDED TO HIS SHOULDER."
"HE'D BEEN OSTRACISED FROM HIS COMMUNITY, BUT NOW HE WAS PROUD TO SUPPORT HIMSELF. ALL THE FARM WORKERS HAD DISABILITIES, BUT THEY PRODUCED GOOD CROPS.
"FUNNY THING IS, SOMEONE HAD BROKEN IN AND STOLEN FROM *THEM*."
"THIS GUY THOUGHT IT WAS HILARIOUS THAT AN ABLE-BODIED PERSON HAD STOLEN FROM THEM."
"HE TOLD ME WHAT HAPPENED THROUGH AN INTERPRETER...
IT WAS LIKE 'SATURDAY NIGHT LIVE'."
"ALL THE TIMING WAS THERE..."
"THE GUY WAS A NATURAL COMEDIAN..."
"AND THE TIME MY WIFE WAS IN A CAB GOING THROUGH HANDSWORTH AT CARNIVAL TIME..."
DOESN'T IT LOOK NICE?
BLOODY DARKIES. SEND 'EM ALL HOME. THEY CAN HAVE AS MANY CARNIVALS AS THEY LIKE, THEN.

MY WIFE WAS FURIOUS...
ACTUALLY, MY HUSBAND IS A "DARKIE"...
QUITE A WELL-KNOWN DARKIE...
TONITE LENNY HENRY
"ALIVE and UNSHEATHED"
ACTUALLY.
LENNY HENRY?
REALLY?
ER... YOU COULDN'T GET US A TICKET?
COULD YOU LOVE?
AND OTHER TIMES... LIKE WHEN MY DAD DIED.
DEATH
REAL-LIFE ·JOLLIES·
THIS WEEK: LEN DEALS WITH A DEATH IN THE FAMILY...
"I'VE LEARNT THAT AS LONG AS I'M ALIVE I'LL NEVER BE SHORT OF MATERIAL...
THE IMPORTANT WOOFS COME FROM MY PAST, MY PRESENT, THINGS I'VE READ, SEEN OR FELT, MY OWN EXPERIENCES."
"I DON'T REALLY KNOW ABOUT ISSUES — ONLY ABOUT WHAT AFFECTS ME. IF THE ISSUE AFFECTS ME... FINE... I'LL GET INVOLVED. BUT DON'T ASK ME TO SPEAK AT ANY RALLIES."
"ALRIGHT."
"TELL ME ABOUT YOUR FATHER INSTEAD."

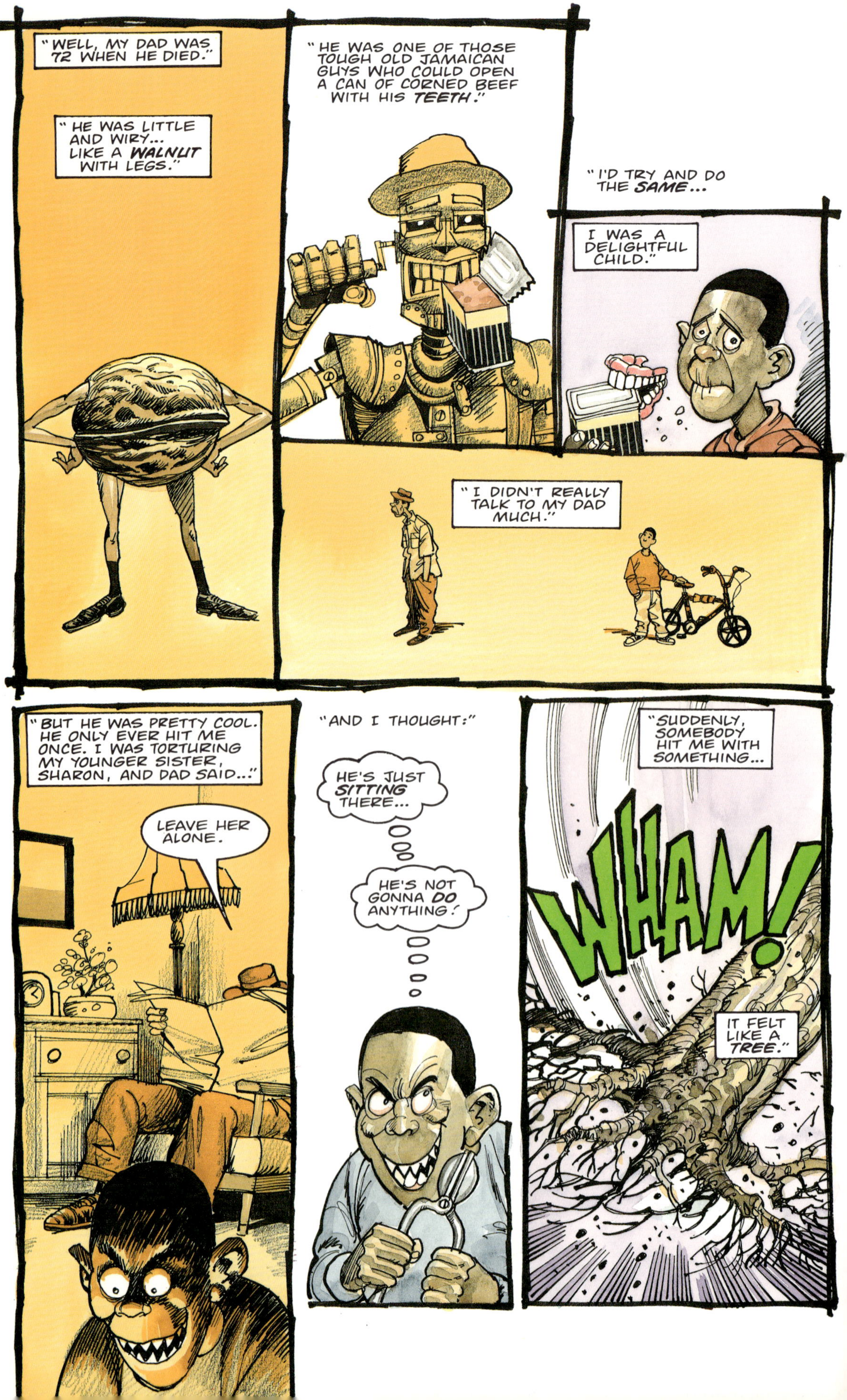
"WELL, MY DAD WAS 72 WHEN HE DIED."
"HE WAS LITTLE AND WIRY... LIKE A WALNUT WITH LEGS."
"HE WAS ONE OF THOSE TOUGH OLD JAMAICAN GUYS WHO COULD OPEN A CAN OF CORNED BEEF WITH HIS TEETH."
"I'D TRY AND DO THE SAME...
I WAS A DELIGHTFUL CHILD."
"I DIDN'T REALLY TALK TO MY DAD MUCH."
"BUT HE WAS PRETTY COOL. HE ONLY EVER HIT ME ONCE. I WAS TORTURING MY YOUNGER SISTER, SHARON, AND DAD SAID..."
LEAVE HER ALONE.
"AND I THOUGHT:"
HE'S JUST SITTING THERE...
HE'S NOT GONNA DO ANYTHING!
"SUDDENLY, SOMEBODY HIT ME WITH SOMETHING...
WHAM!
IT FELT LIKE A TREE."

"AND THEN HE SAID THAT GREAT JAMAICAN DISCIPLINARY PHRASE..."
IF YOU CYAAAN HEAR YOU WILL FEEL.
"MY DAD WAS A SUPERHERO... FORGET THE FLASH... MY DAD WAS...
BLACK LASH
IF YOUR KIDS ARE GIVING YOU HELL, SEND FOR BLACK LASH — HE'LL CLAP THEIR BACKSIDES!"
"DAD USED TO GROW CABBAGES ...BIG CABBAGES ...GREAT GIANT MUTANT CABBAGES...
AND SPUDS...
LOTS OF SPUDS..."
"EVEN THE NEIGHBOURS HAD HAD ENOUGH..."
TELL YOUR DAD THAT HALF A TON OF POTATOES IS MORE THAN GENEROUS!
"HE WORKED IN THE FOUNDRY EVERY DAY...BREATHING IN SMOKE AND FUMES...
HIS LUNGS MUST'VE LOOKED LIKE 'A' SEAM AT KETTLETHORPE COLLIERY."
"MY DAD LOVED TO PLAY DOMINOES...
I DIDN'T UNDERSTAND THE GAME, BUT I KNEW THE RULES..."
"a) FIRST YOU HAVE TO DRINK THE ENTIRE CONTENTS OF A BOTTLE OF JAMAICAN RUM."

b) THEN SLAM THE DOMINOES DOWN AS HARD AS YOU CAN."
SLAM
c) LET OUT AN EAR-PIERCING...
HAH!
AT YOUR OPPONENT.
DAD WAS GREAT AT DOMINOES.
IN 1977 HE WENT INTO HOSPITAL WITH A KIDNEY COMPLAINT.
IT WAS PLAIN TO SEE THE HOSPITAL DIDN'T THINK HE WAS LONG FOR THIS WORLD.
BED AVAILABLE SOON — CALL DEBBIE FOR DETAILS.
"I FOUND MYSELF ASKING HIM ABOUT HIS CHILDHOOD IN JAMAICA."
YAK YAK YAK
YAK YAK
WHAT WERE YOU LIKE AT SCHOOL?
WHAT WAS YOUR FIRST JOB?
WHEN DID YOU MEET MOM?
WAS IT REALLY SNOWING WHEN YOU ARRIVED IN BRITAIN?
YAK
WHO WAS NUMBER—
WHAT IS THIS?
MASTER MIND?
I'VE STARTED, SO I'LL FINISH— WHO WAS NUMBER ONE IN THE HIT PARADE WHEN YOU ARRIVED IN BRITAIN?
"THEY COULD DO NOTHING FOR HIM. HE DIED OF KIDNEY FAILURE, AND VARIOUS OTHER THINGS. TYPICAL JAMAICAN, COULDN'T JUST DIE OF ONE THING, IT HAD TO BE A WHOLE BUNCH OF STUFF."

WHAT'S my DISEASE
MOST JAMAICANS RELISH ILLNESS... IT'S LIKE A GAME.
WELCOME, EVERYBODY TO 'WHAT'S MY DISEASE'! TODAY, OUR PANEL WILL BE GUESSING THE DISEASE OF —
— MRS MURPHY.
MRS MURPHY, YOUR TIME STARTS...
NOW.
WELL, ME HAVE A BACK YOU KNOW, AND THEN THIS PAIN DIG ME IN MY SIDE...
WHEN YOU SEE MY TRIAL, I HAVE A PAIN — IF YOU FEEL IT, YOU CRASH CAR!
SO THE DAY OF THE FUNERAL ARRIVED AND I HADN'T CRIED. IT WAS LIKE SOMEONE HAD SUPER-GLUED MY TEAR DUCTS CLOSED.
AND YOU'RE SUPPOSED TO CRY WHEN YOUR DAD DIES — IT'S ONE OF THE FEW TIMES WHEN MEN ARE ALLOWED TO RELEASE EMOTION.
CRYING IS NOT CONSIDERED WIMPISH WHEN...
a) YOU LOSE THE WORLD CUP...
b) YOUR COMRADE-IN-ARMS IS SHOT...
HE WAS MY SOB BEST BUDGIE...
c) YOUR CAR BREAKS DOWN...
...AND d) WHEN YOU LOSE A MEMBER OF YOUR FAMILY...

THE NEXT THING THAT FREAKED ME OUT WAS THE UNDERTAKERS...
I WALKED INTO THE FUNERAL PARLOUR AND MY DAD WAS LYING IN THIS COFFIN.
HE LOOKED ... RESTED.
HIS SKIN WAS WAXY AND COLD TO THE TOUCH.
I STARED DOWN, WANTING TO ASK HIM A MILLION QUESTIONS.
HEAR HIM SING AN UNKNOWN HARMONY.
LISTEN TO HIM LAUGH...
BUT NO MORE. HE WAS GONE.
AND STILL I DIDN'T CRY.
WE WENT TO THE CHURCH. I DON'T THINK THE VICAR HAD SEEN THAT MANY BLACK PEOPLE...
HE MUST HAVE THOUGHT WE WERE CLAIMING THE LEASE...
I DID NOT KNOW MR. HENRY...
YES, LORD!
BUT THE LORD...
KNOWS HIM!
PRAISE THE LORD!
UM, YES...
PRAISE THE LORD INDEED.

AND THEN THERE WAS SINGING... AND TO HEAR ALL THOSE VOICES IN HARMONY, WELL, YOU SHOULDA BEEN THERE.
THEN WE HAD TO CARRY THE COFFIN OUT, WHICH WAS COOL, BECAUSE MY DAD WAS A LITTLE GUY...
WHAT I WANT TO KNOW IS—WHAT HAPPENED AT ORSON WELLES' FUNERAL?
HEY, LOOK... I DIDN'T KNOW HIM THAT WELL...
WE WEREN'T EXACTLY BOSOM BUDDIES, EITHER.
COULDN'T WE PAY SOMEBODY TO DO THIS?
I AIN'T MOVIN' THAT THANG WITHOUT A FORK-LIFT, YA HEAR?
THE WHOLE CONGREGATION CAME TO THE GRAVESIDE...
SANG HYMNS...
CRIED SOME MORE...
IT WAS UPLIFTING.
PEOPLE FROM OTHER FUNERALS WERE DEFECTING TO US...
LOOK, COULD WE JOIN YOU? OURS IS SO BORING!
THEN IT WAS BACK TO THE HOUSE FOR TEA AND CONVERSATION. POLITICS, SHOWBIZ... GOOD FAMILY STUFF...
ANYWAY, MICHAEL JACKSON'S HAIR IS TOO LONG...
AND HE'S SPOTTY...
HE SHOULD DO SOMETHING ABOUT THAT.
BZZZT
I'LL GET IT.
I WAS A FRIEND OF YOUR FATHER'S.

WELL, IT'S NICE TO MEET YOU, MISTER..?
JOHNSON. UMM...YOU HAVE A DOMINO TABLE?
"AND HE JUST WALKED INTO THE BACK ROOM."
"THEN THE DOORBELL WENT AGAIN. THREE LADIES FROM MOM'S CHURCH..."
WE COME TO KEEP SISTER WINNIE COMPANY.
LADIES, I'M AFRAID MOM'S A BIT UP—
LISTEN, BOY... I COME TO SEE YOUR MOTHER NOT YOU...
BZZZ
NOW HUSH UP!
UHH... YES?
IS CHARLIE HERE?
IN HERE, YOU DAMN IDIOT!
"THEN THE CAKE ARRIVED..."
WHERE IS SISTER WINNIE?
I GIVE IN.
"IT GOT WORSE. THE HYMN SINGING COMPETITION GOT SO LOUD I'M SURE PEOPLE IN CHINA WERE PISSED OFF..."
SOMEBODY MUST'VE DIED IN THE HENRY FAMILY.
YEAH. SOMEONE IS SINGING SHARP THOUGH.
HAH!
"AND OF COURSE, THERE WAS A MAJOR LEAGUE DOMINO TOURNAMENT GOING ON."

"MOM WAS IN THE KITCHEN COOKING FOR THE WHOLE STREET IT SEEMED TO ME..."
MRS. HENRY, HELLO, I'M FROM THREE STREETS AWAY... MY FAMILY AND I WERE WONDERING...
IF WE COULD TRY SOME OF YOUR COW FOOT SOUP?
"AND IN THE FRONT ROOM, THERE WAS ALMOST A DISCO..."
I THINK THE OSMONDS WILL BE HERE FOREVER.
D'YOU THINK FLARES WILL COME BACK INTO FASHION?
I DIDN'T KNOW THEY'D GONE OUT.
WHO SCRATCHED MY VERSION OF SEX MACHINE?
SO, WHAT EXACTLY IS A BABYLON?
"AND MORE AND MORE PEOPLE ARRIVING EVERY MINUTE..."
"THIS IS WHEN I WENT LOOPY."
THAT'S IT! EVERYBODY OUT!
THIS IS A DAY OF MOURNING, NOT A NIGHT OUT!
SOMEBODY'S DIED!
WE'RE SUPPOSED TO BE UNHAPPY!
LEN, STOP!
IT'S NOT FAIR, MOM. THEY'RE TREATING THE HOUSE LIKE A BINGO HALL!

THIS IS A TRADITION... IT GOES BACK TO AFRICA.
PEOPLE CELEBRATE THE DEATH OF A LOVED ONE BY HAVING AN OPEN HOUSE.
THEY CALL IT ALL KINDS OF THINGS.
BUT IN THE WEST INDIES IT'S CALLED THE 9 NIGHTS.
FOR NINE NIGHTS THE RELATIVES AND FRIENDS OF THE DECEASED COME TO THE HOUSE OF THE SURVIVING FAMILY MEMBER AND KEEP THEM OCCUPIED.
THE WIDOW OR WIDOWER HAS TO FIND FOOD AND ENTERTAIN THE GUESTS.
THAT'S NICE. YOU LOSE A LOVED ONE AND HAVE TO BOOK A CABARET.
"NO. IT'S NOT LIKE THAT. THESE PEOPLE ARE HERE OUT OF RESPECT FOR ME AND YOUR FATHER. SO DON'T BE ANGRY. IT'S TRADITION."
AND THAT WAS IT. FOR THE NEXT NINE NIGHTS I HELPED FEED, WATER AND ENTERTAIN THE PEOPLE WHO KNEW AND LOVED MY DAD.
AND ON THE FINAL NIGHT, WHEN THE FIREWOOD HAD BEEN COLLECTED FROM THE DOMINO ROOM... AND THE FINAL SLEEPING DRUNK HOOVERED UP...
I CLIMBED INTO BED... AND CRIED.
AND I HEARD MY DAD'S VOICE IN MY HEAD SAYING...
"BLOODY SISSY..."

THANK YOU VERY MUCH!
YOU'VE BEEN A WONDERFUL AUDIENCE!
CHEER!
WHISTLE!
BRAVO!
YAY!
BRAVO! GREAT STUFF!
BOF
WELL, THANK GOD HE'S GONE!
WELL DONE.
THAT WAS EXCELLENT.
I COULDN'T HAVE DONE IT WITHOUT YOU.
WELL, YOU ARE A QUICK PUPIL, MY BOY...
BUT I MUST BE AWAY!
WHAT? NO!
I'VE GOT ALL KINDS OF THINGS I NEED TO KNOW!
AND YOU WILL...
JUST KEEP DOING WHAT YOU'RE DOING.
DON'T WORRY ABOUT WOOFS. TELL THE STORY... GET INVOLVED.
SOMETIMES THE BEST THING TO DO WITH A WOOF... IS TO TAKE IT OUT!
THANKS, MAN... WHERE WILL YOU GO NOW?
MY DEAR CHAP, YOU'RE NOT THE ONLY COMEDIAN IN THE UNIVERSE WITH WOOF TROUBLE Y'KNOW.
SNAP
'BYE!
BOF

MEANWHILE, ON THE PLANET DWEEB...
TAP TAP TAP
TAP TAP TAP TAP TAP
SKRIT
TOK
AGGHH
BING BONG

the LAST WORD...

AS I GOT MORE EXPERIENCE, MY RESPONSES TO HECKLER FIRE BECAME SHARPER...
JAPE GRENADES.
GAG MANUAL.
RUBBER CHICKEN: "IF IN DOUBT, SHOW 'EM YOUR COCK."
I WAS EQUIPPED.
WHAT A CRAP SUIT!
CALL THIS AN ACT?
SIT BACK IN YOUR CHAIR, PAL...
WE'LL PLUG IT IN!
WHO WRITES YOUR JOKES? NOAH?
WE GET YOU ON OUR TELLY AT HOME—
—INTERFERENCE!
WOOF
SO, EQUIPPED WITH MORE VERBAL FIREPOWER THAN IS FAIR, COMEDIANS GO OUT INTO THE CIVILIAN WORLD...
LAUGHOCET MISSILES.
GIGGLE GUNS.
CHUCKLE GAS.
READY TO TROUNCE ANY JERK WHO DARES TO CRINKLE TOFFEE PAPER...
OR GO TO THE TOILET IN THE MIDDLE OF A JOKE.

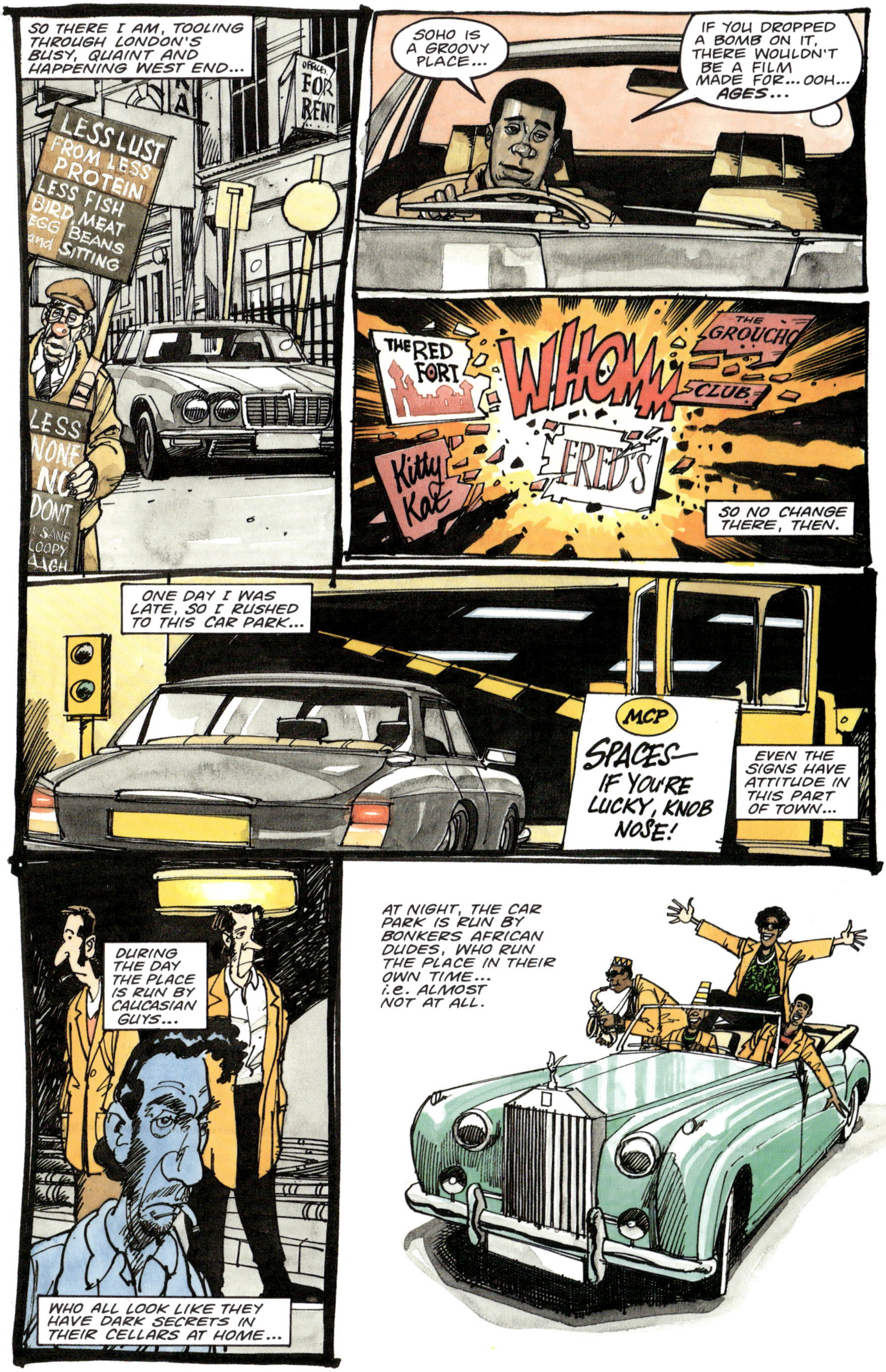

SO THERE I AM, TOOLING THROUGH LONDON'S BUSY, QUAINT AND HAPPENING WEST END...
LESS LUST FROM LESS PROTEIN LESS FISH BIRD MEAT EGG BEANS and SITTING
OFFICES FOR RENT
SOHO IS A GROOVY PLACE...
IF YOU DROPPED A BOMB ON IT, THERE WOULDN'T BE A FILM MADE FOR... OOH... AGES...
THE RED FORT
WHOMM
THE GROUCHO CLUB
Kitty Kat
FRED'S
SO NO CHANGE THERE, THEN.
ONE DAY I WAS LATE, SO I RUSHED TO THIS CAR PARK...
MCP
SPACES— IF YOU'RE LUCKY, KNOB NOSE!
EVEN THE SIGNS HAVE ATTITUDE IN THIS PART OF TOWN...
DURING THE DAY THE PLACE IS RUN BY CAUCASIAN GUYS...
WHO ALL LOOK LIKE THEY HAVE DARK SECRETS IN THEIR CELLARS AT HOME...
AT NIGHT, THE CAR PARK IS RUN BY BONKERS AFRICAN DUDES, WHO RUN THE PLACE IN THEIR OWN TIME... i.e. ALMOST NOT AT ALL.

MY WIFE USES THIS CAR PARK AND HEARD A DAYTIME DUDE REFER TO ONE OF THE AFRICANS AS "A BLEEDIN' SPADE".
SO AS I DROVE IN I WAS READY.
ATTITUDE
'ERE, LEN. SIGN THESE FOR THE KIDS WILL YA?
NO PROBLEM.
I KNOW, IT'S NOT FOR YOU. IT'S FOR THE WIFE.
'OY!'
WHAT'S A BLACK GEEZER DOIN' WIV A MOTOR LIKE THIS THEN?
"THIS IS WHERE ALL THOSE YEARS OF TRAINING CAME INTO PLAY. I WAS ARMED WITH ENOUGH VERBAL WEAPONRY TO DEMOLISH CAESAR'S PALACE, LUTON. THIS GUY WAS DOGMEAT. I CHOSE MY WORDS CAREFULLY...
FLIPPED THROUGH MY MENTAL FILING CABINET OF PUT-DOWNS, PITHY REJOINDERS AND DEVASTATING ONE-LINERS..."

"SUDDENLY..."
FUCK
TOUGH LUCK. IT DOESN'T WORK ALL THE TIME.
39
WHUP
WHUP
WHUP
FIN
PARK HOUSE '91